DARA G

A

Gentleman's
Offer

KIMANI
ROMANCE

To my readers

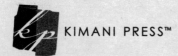 KIMANI PRESS™

ISBN-13: 978-0-373-86085-2
ISBN-10:   0-373-86085-4

A GENTLEMAN'S OFFER

www.kimanipress.com

Printed in U.S.A.

"You give orders very well," Nate said.

"Thank you. When you work with animals you realize the importance of being firm. They respect those who are in charge." She winked at him. "Plus I just wanted to try out my new role."

"I bet you'll enjoy ordering me around. You've started off with the right attitude."

Yes, she'd definitely love to order him around. She would begin with having him remove his shirt, then his trousers, then his... She adjusted her position. What were they talking about again? Oh yes, attitude. "Is that said with approval or censure?"

"What would you like it to be?"

"Approval." She waved her finger. "And I know what you're going to say. That the rich don't care what anyone else thinks."

Nate stretched out his leg and it brushed hers. She didn't move; neither did he. She took a deep breath, reminding herself that it was no big deal.

He looked at her with a steady gaze. "Yes?" His leg brushed hers again, sending an electric current through her. This time she knew it wasn't an accident. That only made it more distracting.

Books by Dara Girard

Kimani Romance

Sparks
The Glass Slipper Project

Kimani Arabesque

Table for Two
Gaining Interest
Carefree
Illusive Flame

DARA GIRARD

is an award-winning author of both fiction and nonfiction books. Her love of writing started at a young age. After graduating from college, she decided to write full-time. She enjoys writing romance because of the range it provides, from comedy to suspense. Her novels are known for their sense of humor, interesting plot twists and witty dialogue.

In addition to writing novels, Dara enjoys reading, painting and going for long drives.

Dara loves hearing from her readers. You can contact her at www.daragirard.com or P.O. Box 10345, Silver Spring, Maryland 20914.

Dear Reader,

Welcome to the second book in THE BLACK
STOCKINGS SOCIETY series.

What would you do with a million dollars? That was
the premise on which I based *A Gentleman's Offer*. Does
money really change people, and can true love rise above
deception?

Artsy Yvette Coulier and straitlaced Nate Blackwell answer
this question for me. Both characters provided me with
ample space to introduce adventure and romance. Nate
learns that Yvette is more of a lady than she seems and
Nate proves to be just the man to make *all* of Yvette's
dreams come true.

Both learn the magic of love.

I hope you enjoy Yvette and Nate's story. If you'd like to
learn about my other titles, please visit my Web site at
www.daragirard.com.

All the best,

Dara Girard

Chapter 1

"Is that groomer girl still here?" Mrs. Penny Kerner asked her daughter in a loud voice, adjusting the collar of her suede jacket, while looking at herself in a large hallway mirror.

Her daughter, Cathleen, having a more gentle nature and softer tone replied in a whisper, "Mother, lower your voice. She's right around the corner and may hear you." Cathleen glanced anxiously toward a door that was partially ajar.

"I don't care."

Cathleen raised her tone a bit. "Besides, she's not a groomer, she's a pet stylist."

"She's a dog groomer. A fancy name doesn't change what she does."

"I'm sure they'll be done soon."

"I hope so," her mother stated harshly.

Yvette Coulier continued to brush the luxuriously silky brown fur of Binky, a three-year-old Pomeranian, as she sat snugly in the folds of an oversize, blue crushed-velvet cushion. She had been very cooperative and had managed to maintain the same position throughout the photo shoot. Although the photographer, Lewis Wolfson, had finished taking pictures, Yvette wanted to make sure that Binky continued to look her best. Not that Binky didn't already match the elegance of the Kerner's mansion with its vaulted ceilings, Mediterranean marble floors and a life-size oil painting of Mrs. Kerner and Cathleen that dominated the main foyer. Yvette wanted to spend just a little more time. She could hear the soothing sound of the waterfall sculpture coming from the open patio door. It was an unseasonably warm spring for Michigan and Mrs. Kerner had insisted that she wanted "natural" air flowing through the house.

Mrs. Kerner was right. She was just a dog groomer. Perhaps one of the best in the city, but a groomer all the same. However, Yvette wasn't ashamed of her job and took great pride in what she did. She'd started volunteering at animal shelters while in high school and had had a brief stint as a vet tech, before becoming a grooming assistant at a local salon. Four years later she partnered with her friend Madlyn to open Le Chic Hounds, and very soon her reputation grew. In just a few years, Yvette had groomed the dogs of both major and minor celebrities, socialites and very rich bachelors. And although she got invited to some outrageously expensive homes, she always felt out of place. Her job allowed her to mingle with a class of people with whom she knew she'd never belong, but secretly desired to.

"I just had a thought," Lewis said as he put his camera equipment away. He was a large, handsome man of thirty with dark brown bedroom eyes and a boyish smile.

Yvette began to pack her supplies as well. "What?"

"Our lives suck."

She sent him a censoring glance. "Speak for yourself."

"Look at us." He gestured to them, then the room. "The only reason we're in this fabulous mansion is for a three-year-old dog!"

"Pomeranian," she corrected.

"The breed doesn't matter."

"The breed *always* matters."

"Well, whatever breed he happens to be, you're grooming him and I'm taking his picture. Doesn't that seem odd to you?"

"*She's* keeping us fed." Yvette shrugged. "Besides, other people aren't this lucky."

Lewis stared at her, incredulous. "You call this lucky?"

"At least we're not sweeping floors."

Lewis took several steps forward, motioning to Binky, who by now was ready to take a nap. "This dog is wearing a collar that's half my salary. Do you notice how she doesn't even move?"

"She's well trained."

"I bet she gets picked up so much she doesn't even know how to walk." He closed a large case.

"I'm sure she walks just fine, but I did notice that her paws are a little tender."

Lewis frowned at the dog. "From what I see she's not suffering and she certainly has a better life than I do."

Yvette shook her head. "You're getting depressed again."

"I'm already depressed."

Yvette sent Lewis a questioning look. "You and Tansin split up again?"

He shoved his hands in his jeans pockets. "It's over this time."

"Uh-huh," Yvette said, unconvinced.

"For good."

"You've broken up seven times in as many months. I'll wait before I say I'm sorry for you."

"I'm telling you the absolute truth." He winked at her. "Now I'm a free man."

Yvette shook her head. "It would never work. You're not my type."

"Nobody's your type. I've never seen you express interest in a man, or even a woman."

"I'm not into women." She zipped up her bag.

Lewis raised his hands in surrender. "I had wondered."

"Well, now you can stop wondering."

He folded his arms. "So you like men?"

"Sure."

"Then how come after knowing you for most of your life I don't know what type of man would catch your interest?" He snapped his fingers. "Wait. I know the perfect man for you."

"Who?"

"Someone really old and very rich. You'd make the perfect kept woman."

Yvette thought it best not to reply. Lewis wasn't the only man to think so. Men liked Yvette—young men, old men, plain men, handsome men, single men and unfortunately, married men. Especially married men. Men who thought she'd be the perfect mistress. She had had two short-lived semi-serious relationships in her early twenties but that was all. She didn't need a man anyway. At twenty-eight she felt her life was on track and she was perfectly happy on her own.

Yvette owned a fashionable dog-grooming business. But although she was doing well, she had a long way to go to earn the kind of income that would elevate her to the status she dreamed of.

"I was supposed to be the next Gordon Parks," Lewis said with a weary sigh. "Or Ansel Adams. But look at me."

Yvette looked at him and wanted to laugh. Lewis could never look like a tragic figure. He was too well dressed. He always wore name-brand clothes and had a new watch every three months. Yvette never asked him how he was able to afford his purchases, although she was curious.

"You're still young enough to make your mark," she said, refusing to offer any sympathy. "Everybody has to pay their bills. People understand that."

"Tansin didn't."

"Don't blame Tansin for your lack of success. Besides, she probably isn't right for you."

He raised a sly brow. "You might be right for me."

"We already addressed that topic."

"I was hoping you'd changed your mind."

"I haven't."

He sat on the couch, brushing away a large leaf from a palm tree next to him.

Yvette sent a nervous glance toward the doorway. "Get up. You're not supposed to look as though you're relaxing."

"I'm sitting down. Besides, this chair is far from relaxing. It's probably softer on the floor."

"Then sit on the floor."

"You care too much about what they think."

"Yes, because my reputation is everything."

"I'll get up when I hear them coming. You should sit down, too. You've been fussing over that dog for hours."

Yvette was used to being on her feet, but knew this grueling job would have her soaking in a bath tonight.

Lewis wagged a finger at her. "One day someone is going to make you change your mind about your ideal man."

"I don't have an ideal."

"Everybody has an ideal. You just don't know yours. You know what your problem is?"

"The fact that you won't stop talking?"

He shook his head. "No. You just don't like people. You only associate with animals. And yet you don't even have a pet."

"I don't have the time."

"You never make time for relationships in your life."

Yvette rested her hands on her hips and looked at him, annoyed. "Why are we talking about me? I thought you were the one who's miserable."

"I am. I'm just trying to convince you that you are, too."

She made a face.

The sound of footsteps coming in their direction made Lewis jump up. Yvette adjusted Binky's diamond-encrusted collar.

Penny entered the room with Cathleen trailing behind her. Penny had a fat neck, which she couldn't help, but she made the unfortunate decision of emphasizing it with large, expensive jewelry, either because she was ignorant of her flaw or vain. Cathleen, who couldn't be older than twenty-three, nearly disappeared behind her mother in a green silk dress that was obviously expensive but two sizes too big. From what she'd observed, Yvette had an uneasy feeling that Penny spent most of her money and attention on Binky, instead of her daughter.

"Are we all finished now?" Penny said in a voice that implied that they were.

Lewis swung his camera bag over his shoulder. "Yes."

She picked Binky up. "Don't we look beautiful?"

"She was very good," Yvette said.

"Naturally."

"She really looks nice," Cathleen said, reaching out to stroke Binky. Penny slapped her hand away. Cathleen withdrew her hand, looking embarrassed, and stared at the floor.

Yvette glanced at Lewis who only shrugged. She glanced at Binky's paws then cleared her throat. "May I make a suggestion?"

"No," Penny responded, as she continued fussing over the dog.

"Yes," a deep voice said from the doorway. Yvette and Lewis turned their attention to a tall, dark figure. Most contemporary men weren't built like him. They'd been sensitized, refined. He was a throwback to a different era, even in his black suit. His movements were too coarse to be called cultured and his body to large to be called elegant. Yet he was both. And then there was his face. *Handsome* seemed too simple a word to describe him for his features were both sharp and tender, fine but not delicate and there was an inherent strength about him. It was without the haughty veneer of most attractive men. Yvette had never gasped at the sight of a man before. She was too practical for that, but for some reason this man made breathing seem difficult. Especially when he stepped from the doorway and approached them. His compelling brown eyes briefly met hers across the room, sending unwanted shivers of awareness through her.

Penny turned to him. "But she's just a—"

The man sent her a cutting glance and she stopped, for a moment looking just as chastised as her daughter had been earlier. He turned his piercing gaze to Yvette. "Please continue, Miss…" He made an impatient gesture with his hand demanding that she fill in the blank.

"Coulier," Yvette dutifully answered.

He nodded. "My aunt can always benefit from good advice."

Penny didn't look as though any advice would be welcome. Her lips practically disappeared into her mouth, and her skin, previously a nice warm beige, was an unhealthy shade of red. However, Yvette maintained her composure. She kept her voice firm. "I just wanted to suggest that you change your floor polish."

Penny sent her a cold glare, the red in her cheeks becoming more prominent. "I don't clean floors."

"Right. Sure," Yvette said quickly. "You need to tell your housekeeper. I noticed some tender areas on Binky's paws, which may mean that she's allergic to what's being used to clean your floors. Of course, there could be another reason for the sensitivity she's experiencing. It appears that she prefers to be carried rather than walk."

"Fascinating," the stranger said.

"I already knew that," Penny retorted, displaying her irritation with a brief roll of her eyes.

The stranger's reply came as a soft challenge. "Did you?"

Penny bristled at the implication. "Yes, but thank you anyway."

"You're welcome," Yvette said, amazed at the command this man had over Mrs. Kerner, although he was many years younger.

Penny turned and headed for the door. "Thank you for coming. Hanson will give you your money on the way out."

Yvette turned to thank the stranger but he'd disappeared through the patio doors.

"We've been dismissed," Lewis said, picking up his items.

"Be quiet," Yvette said, squashing her disappointment that she hadn't had a chance to talk to the mysterious man. She looked at the young woman who still stood quietly staring at the ground.

"He's right, you know," Cathleen said lifting her head. She offered a shy smile. "Mother isn't always tactful and Nate's just…well, Nate."

Lewis adjusted the strap of his bag. "Hey, as long as she pays, I don't care how she acts."

Yvette walked up to Cathleen, surprised that she would speak without permission. Since their arrival earlier that morning, Cathleen had been her mother's shadow or had stood about looking at the ground. She held out her hand. "We never got a chance to introduce ourselves. I'm Yvette."

Yvette jerked her head in Lewis's direction as he inched his way toward the door, eager to leave. "He's Lewis."

Lewis waved over his shoulder, not wanting to spend any more time than necessary, unless of course, he could bill for it.

"If you have other family or friends with dogs I hope you will mention us." She handed Cathleen a stack of business cards.

"Sure."

Yvette then picked up her equipment bag and left.

Moments later she and Lewis sat outside a restaurant eating their lunch. They'd left the pricey enclave of Crystal Hills, knowing that their money wouldn't go far in the restaurants and cafés there. They now sat in the heart of Detroit. As an adventurous pair they liked to sample the exotic culinary diversions the city offered like Hungarian, Greek, Indian, Caribbean or Italian. Today they chose American. The sounds of honking, roaring engines, loud rap music clashing with rock guitars coming through car windows and people rushing past faded into the background.

Yvette removed several turkey slices from her sandwich and wrapped them up in a napkin.

Lewis frowned. "I wish you'd stop doing that."

"They always give me too much. This is enough for two people!"

"Feeding the homeless is like feeding the rat population. It only makes them spread."

"Humans and rodents are very different. Excuse me." Yvette darted across the street and approached a homeless man sitting on the pavement. She knew him only as "Corner" and his dog as "Runt". "It's turkey today," she said, handing him the wrapped meat.

"Runt loves turkey. Thank you."

She nodded, then returned back to her table.

Lewis frowned at her. "Happy now?"

"Very."

"How much did you give him?"

"A few slices."

"How much money did you put with those slices?"

"None of your business."

"You don't like people, but you feed your lunch to a dog and give money to a guy who doesn't work."

"I like anyone who cares about animals. Besides, Runt is his friend."

He bit into a french fry. "I doubt that girl back at the mansion has any friends," Lewis said. "Hell, she can't even pet her own dog. You wasted a bunch of business cards."

"No I didn't and it doesn't hurt to ask. She might know someone who could use us." Yvette sipped her drink, unaware of the admiring glances cast in her direction. It wasn't that she was oblivious of her looks and how they affected others; she was just disinterested, which only added an air of mystery. She was a natural beauty with defined facial features, smoky gray-brown eyes and long dark hair, which she had highlighted with bold blond streaks. Her jeans and T-shirt emphasized her slender build while three studs dotted one ear and four pierced the other. Her French-Canadian mother liked to hold claim to her walnut skin and elegant features, while her Jamaican father said that her inner spirit was from him.

"So what are we going to do about it?" Lewis asked.

"About what?"

"Our pathetic lives."

"I wish you'd stop including me in your equation."

"We're friends. We share everything, even misery."

"I'm not miserable."

He crumbled up his hamburger wrapper. "I saw you looking at Cathleen. Different parents and that could have been you."

"I don't think so. I felt sorry for her. Could you imagine having a mother like that?"

Lewis sat back. "Could you imagine living in a house like that? And don't pretend that the idea hasn't crossed your mind. I bet you would have liked that guy to have looked at you instead of walking past."

"What guy?" Yvette knew who he was referring to, but wanted to pretend that she didn't. She'd already thought about him at least twenty times. Why had he listened to what she'd said, then left so quickly?

"The guy you couldn't stop staring at. Neil."

"His name is Nate and I wasn't staring. I was just paying attention."

"You never pay that much attention. If you

had Cathleen's money he would have given you a second look, but as one of the servants he didn't even stay to say goodbye."

"I'm not a servant. Besides, he looked like he was in a hurry."

"Didn't seem like he was in a hurry to me. I wonder what he does all day? Did you see the waterfall?"

"Yes. If we work hard, one day we'll be able to live in a house like that."

Lewis shook his head. "That's an American myth. We couldn't work hard enough. We'd better start playing the lottery or marry rich."

"I could never marry for money."

Lewis suddenly looked thoughtful. "Why not?"

"Because I'd regret it."

"What is there to regret? Regret is for people who think too much. Imagine if you married someone with money. Right now you'd be eating lobster and caviar. You could—"

"I still wouldn't marry for it."

"You've had offers."

"And I've said no."

"If I were a woman, I would. It's easier for women that way. Men are supposed to provide."

"I want my own money."

"So what if it's his money? You're a goody-

goody, although you hate to admit it. Think of what you could do." He glanced across the street to Corner, who was feeding Runt a slice of turkey. "He's a drunk you know."

"I know," she said in a quiet voice. Her father had been one, too, for years. He'd doused that inner fire he claimed she had with beer and rum. His drinking hadn't scared her much as a child because his disposition remained the same. It was when he couldn't pay a bill, or when he asked her and her sister to persuade the landlord for an extension on their rent so their mother wouldn't find out that he hadn't paid and had spent the money instead, that frightened her.

Fortunately, he finally sobered up after her mother threatened to leave him and take her and her sister, too. From then on their lives improved and their utilities were no longer cut off and bill collectors no longer appeared on their doorstep. But as she stared at Corner, Yvette knew she would never depend on a man to take care of her. She took a final sip of her drink. "I'd hate to be bound to someone in order to get money. I don't want to be a kept woman."

Lewis lifted his plastic cup in a mock toast. "Suit yourself."

Yvette looked away and caught a glimpse of something that nearly broke her heart.

Chapter 2

Tied to a street lamppost with a dirty piece of rope was an unkempt dog.

It looked miserable. At first Yvette couldn't tell what breed it was supposed to be. It had the sad look of a bloodhound mixed with a boxer who had just lost a fight. Its fur was lackluster, thick and matted in places although it was a short-haired breed, and its movements were awkward and painful from nails that were obviously overgrown.

Lewis caught her glance and groaned. "Yvette, leave it," he warned, knowing she hated seeing any animal mistreated, especially dogs. But she couldn't. Yvette got up from the table and approached the middle-aged woman who sat near the dog drinking a cup of coffee. Thick glasses made her eyes look like pin dots and a green hat fell low over her forehead, shielding her face.

"Excuse me, my name is, Yvette." She handed the woman her card, then looked at the dog. "I love dogs. What's his name?"

"James and I'm Margaret." The woman placed a hand on her chest. Her skin looked clean but her nails were filthy.

"Nice to meet you both. Is he a Boston terrier?"

The woman shrugged. "I don't know."

"They are a very handsome breed when they're groomed. They're known as 'The American Gentleman' because of their black-and-white markings, like him." Yvette made a sweeping motion indicating the markings. "I'm sure when he's all cleaned up he'll look like he's wearing a tuxedo. I am telling you this because we're having a grooming special at Le Chic Hounds."

"Le Chic Hounds?" Margaret repeated, unsure.

Yvette tried not to grimace. Madlyn had

decided on the name although Yvette had argued
that a faux French name could be misleading.
She'd been wrong, business was booming. "Yes,
and we always have specials."

Margaret glanced at the card with interest.
"Really? How much?"

Yvette quoted an obscenely low price, but
the woman still hesitated. "I have an opening
today," she added.

Lewis, who was behind her, groaned. Yvette
ignored him and pulled out a chair, its metal legs
scraping against the concrete sidewalk. She sat.
"Just tell me a little bit about James. Is he
neutered?"

"Yes."

"Good." Yvette asked a few more questions
then asked, "Do you think you could come and
see me today, say in an hour? I can give you the
directions from here. It's not too far."

"Well, I suppose I can't pass up a special."

Yvette drew a map on a napkin then stood.
"I'll see you soon."

"Yes."

Yvette returned to her table to clean up.

Lewis shook his head. "Madlyn is going to kill
you."

"She's not coming in until later. She won't
know."

Unfortunately, the moment Yvette arrived at the store, she knew she was in trouble. The upscale dog boutique was having a slow day and looking through the large display window she could see her partner, Madlyn Garcia Tempwood, organizing the large array of pet pillows and matching outfits. Madlyn, who'd grown up privileged, owned the front of the business, which was a doggie boutique.

She and Madlyn were business partners but more acquaintances than friends. Although at times Yvette liked to provoke her by referring to Madlyn as a "you-fer" because she spent her childhood in the Upper Peninsula of Michigan, which was full of tourist areas and parks. Madlyn in turn would mention Yvette's Lower Peninsula roots when she wanted to make a reference to anything that was lowbrow and dirty. It wasn't a vicious rivalry, just part of their Michigan blood. Not only did their upbringings differ, so did their taste.

Madlyn had decorated the boutique after a 1930s salon with retro images and colors. Few items had price tags. Her favorite motto was that if someone had to ask how much something was, they didn't belong there. Madlyn fit in perfectly with the décor with her dramatic eye makeup, loud jewelry and A-line polyester dress. Yvette knew she wouldn't be able to sneak her new client into the grooming salon without being noticed.

She swore.

Lewis laughed. "Told you."

"Don't you have some film to develop?"

"Later. I find this more interesting."

"You could distract her."

"She can smell an imposter."

"Why don't you take her through the back door?"

"Because it's broken. It's being repaired tomorrow."

"We're here!"

They both turned and looked at the new arrivals. Margaret and James looked pathetic and out of place standing there in the elegant neighborhood, which was just a few minutes outside the city.

Yvette glanced inside again. "I can do this."

Margaret looked worried. "Is there a problem?"

"No, just follow closely behind Lewis. Very closely."

"Okay."

Lewis began to protest but Yvette sent him a look and he sighed and mouthed, "This won't work." Yvette entered first, Lewis soon after.

Madlyn was adjusting a collection of doggie bags as Lewis shuttled Margaret and James to the curtain leading to the grooming salon.

"Yvette, I need to speak with you," Madlyn said without taking her gaze off the bags.

Yvette stopped, shrugged at Lewis and whispered, "Just meet me in the back," then walked up to Madlyn. "Hi. What happened to your meeting?"

She lifted a bag and examined its handle. "It was canceled." She replaced the bag on the hook. "What just followed you in here?"

"A client."

"Then why does she look like a pet owner?"

There were two types of people Madlyn didn't like—cheap people and pet owners. The clients she serviced didn't consider their animals "pets." They were part of the family. Pet owners were people who could not or would not be able to afford her exorbitant fees.

"I'll handle her."

Madlyn straightened. She was a foot shorter than Yvette, but held herself tall. "What homeless woman did she rob to get that coat? And did you see her hair?"

"Madlyn."

"And that dog! I bet it has never been inside a grooming salon before. My God, there will be fleas everywhere."

"He doesn't have fleas."

"I bet he does. She doesn't look like she's been to a groomer before, either."

"There's a first time for everything."

Madlyn turned to Yvette, her pretty olive-toned skin an uncomplimentary purple. "Are you trying to make us look bad? Do you know how hard I have worked to develop our reputation?"

"Yes."

"I hope I don't have to remind you of how you were discovered."

Madlyn—not one for modesty—liked to consider herself the one who had plucked Yvette out of obscurity and helped build her name. Although Madlyn had given Yvette key contacts, and had contributed more money to the business venture, while Yvette gave sweat equity, she wished she didn't remind her of that fact every time she was annoyed with her.

Yvette envied Madlyn's status. She mingled easily with the upper classes and her name meant something. Yvette's name meant a good dog cut and nothing more. No matter what she did, no one really noticed Yvette the way they did Madlyn.

Yvette switched her bag to her other arm. "I'll hurry her out once I'm done. No one will notice."

Madlyn smoothed out a crease on Yvette's sleeve. "Fine, but I warn you. Stop picking up strays." She raised a brow. "You don't make money by always offering discounts to people who can't pay."

Yvette left Madlyn and the quiet elegance of the boutique and entered the noisy chaos of the grooming salon where her assistants were busy at work. There was a cacophony of sounds: running water, blow-dryers, electric shavers and barking dogs. Light shone through the large windows, polishing the steel tables and sinks.

"Short scissors!" she told one inexperienced young man as he prepared to trim a poodle. "Mind the quick," she told another groomer, cutting the toenails of a Great Dane. "I don't want you cutting through the blood supply." She finally looked at Margaret, who sat in the corner scribbling something down in a black book. James, the Boston terrier, looked even more miserable, sitting beside her.

"Your friend left."

Yvette clapped her hands together in a cheerful manner. "That's okay. I don't need him." She pulled out a chair from behind her desk, which looked very worn, but comfortable, and sat. "He doesn't appreciate my office." Yvette gestured to the noisy room. "Now, I can get to work."

"She doesn't want me here," Margaret said, referring to Madlyn.

Yvette waved her hand in a dismissive gesture. "Don't worry about her." She knelt down in front of James. "Now I'm going to make you into the handsome little Boston terrier you're supposed to be." She glanced at the small notebook on Margaret's lap. "I thought only men carried little black books," she teased.

Margaret suddenly looked sly. "Little black books are powerful things. I keep lots of notes. Are you married?"

Yvette considered lying. She didn't want to be set up with anyone. "I'm married to my work."

"So you like what you do?"

Yvette nodded. "Very much."

"And do you want to get married?"

Yvette picked up a pen. "I'd rather be rich."

"Money can be cold comfort."

She began filling out a form with James's information. "Money can buy you comfort."

Margaret frowned. "You really believe that?"

Yvette placed her pen down. "Yes. I don't mean to sound shallow, but money gives you privileges that ordinary people don't have. A man may give you status, but money gives you power."

"What about love?"

"My family loves me. That's enough."

Margaret looked thoughtful, then nodded and wrote some more notes in her book before

tucking it away in her purse. "I have to be somewhere in a few minutes. Can I pick James up
later?"

"Yes, or we can have him delivered."

"No, that won't be necessary. I trust you with
him."

After Margaret left, Greg, Yvette's main assistant, looked at James with pity. "Want me to do
him?"

"No, he gets the special treatment." Yvette
immediately went about doing what she did
best—washing, trimming and hand blow-drying
James. At the end he looked like a new dog. His
black-and-white coat gleamed.

"A true gentleman," she proudly announced as
she placed him in a cage nearby. All of a sudden
she found herself thinking about Nate standing in
the doorway, the commanding way he spoke and
moved. He'd look devastating in a tuxedo. She
brushed the thought aside. She didn't think about
men, didn't have time for them. Besides, he
hadn't shown any interest in her. She was used to
men looking at her, and giving the once-over, but
he hadn't done that. Unlike so many of the
handsome, rich men who couldn't take their eyes
off her, he didn't seem to notice that she existed.
She patted James on the head. "Just wait until
Margaret sees you."

Unfortunately, Margaret hadn't returned by the close of business, so Yvette left herself a note to call the next day. She took a moment to make sure James was comfortable by putting a soft blanket and some doggie toys in his cage. She didn't have to worry; he was fast asleep. She turned off the lights and left. Yvette lived in an old two-story brownstone with three other tenants. The moment she entered the foyer she saw that the landlady, Mrs. Cantrell, had her apartment door open. Yvette groaned. Rarely could she pass by undetected. She raced up the stairs, but stepped on a board that creaked and Mrs. Cantrell—a woman with a small mouth and a loud voice—appeared in the doorway.

"There you are! I was hoping to see you."

"Really?" Yvette said without surprise.

"It's my poor Lancelot. I think he has an eye infection."

"Then you should take him to a vet."

"I'd rather you see him first."

"I'm not a vet."

"But you know a lot about dogs."

Yvette glanced longingly up the stairs. "I really have to—"

"Just one look. I saw some clear liquid coming out of his eye."

Yvette sighed. *They were probably tears,*

because the poor creature knew there was no escape. She turned around, started back down the stairs, and followed Mrs. Cantrell into the apartment. Knickknacks and pictures choked the apartment from the living room to the kitchen. Then she saw a man sitting on the couch. The moment Mrs. Cantrell closed the door Yvette knew she'd fallen into a trap.

Chapter 3

"I don't like leaving you alone."

Nate Blackwell sat on the couch in his sister's elegant apartment and watched her pace in front of him. She rarely paced and she rarely worried about anything—except him. He tried to ease her anxiety with a smile. "I'm not alone." He gestured to the two dogs near his feet. "I have King and Queen to keep me company."

"Still…are you sure you don't want to come with me?" She stopped pacing and stared at him. "I could get a sitter."

"Diana, I'll be fine. Stop worrying about me."

She returned to pacing, this time flexing and unflexing her fingers. "Don't forget Queen's appointment. It took me forever to get on Yvette's schedule. She runs the salon and usually lets her assistants do the work, but I asked for her specifically because she's the best."

"Fine."

"I would have gotten Jenny to take her, but it's her day off."

"Fine."

"So remember—"

Nate got up from the couch and seized Diana's wrist as she passed him, forcing her to stop and look at him. He grinned. "I'll remember."

She hesitated. "Kim was asking about you."

He released her wrist and his grin fell. "You didn't tell her where I was, did you?"

"No, but she wants to talk to you."

"So what?"

"Last year was—"

He sat back down and stretched out his legs, nudging King, who rolled onto his back for a belly rub. Nate obliged him using his foot. "I don't want to talk about it."

"I know it was hard for you, but it was hard for us, too."

He bent down and rubbed King's belly with his hand.

Diana sat next to him. "Where were you anyway?"

"Tormenting Aunt Penny."

"Leave her alone."

"Why?" He sat back and folded his arms. King remained on his back a few moments then, realizing his massage was finished, rolled over and went to sleep. "I don't come to visit often."

"Why do you enjoy making her uncomfortable?"

He winked at her. "Because I can." He shook his head. "You should have seen her today trying to eat up some little dog groomer."

Diana lifted a sly brow. "Was she pretty?"

"Sure, but she's not my type."

"Why not?"

"I don't go for blond streaks and artistic outfits."

Diana jumped. "That's Yvette! And she's more than pretty, she's gorgeous." Diana frowned. "I hope you were nice to her." She held her hands together as though pleading. "Please tell me you were nice to her."

"*I* was nice to her. It was Aunty Penny who could have ruined things for you. As I said, she was trying to bully her just because she had an opinion."

Diana waved a dismissive hand. "Yvette can handle Aunt Penny, that's why I recommended her for the job."

"Aunt Penny would have eaten her for dinner if she could have."

Diana crossed her legs and smoothed her skirt. "You stopped her of course."

"Of course. She made sense. She seems to be a smart woman."

"You sound surprised."

"Let's just say I didn't expect someone with that many piercings, who likes to clean dogs, to sound that educated. But I was wrong and I'm glad I made Aunt Penny listen."

Diana shook her head. "You shouldn't keep doing that."

"Doing what?"

"Coming to a woman's rescue. Haven't you ever heard of the white knight?"

"I'm no white knight."

"Remember how you met Kim?"

Nate stood and turned on the radio. "I don't want to talk about her."

Diana lifted the remote and turned it off. "You helped her brother's company out of bankruptcy."

He shoved his hands in his pockets. "So what?" He kept his back to her and looked out the window.

"One day you're going to rescue a woman and find yourself in deep trouble."

He shrugged. "I'm not afraid."

"I'm serious, Nate. Stop rescuing women."

"Don't worry. I'm on vacation." He turned to her with a smug grin. "What could happen?"

Yvette sat next to two hundred and fifty pounds of moving flesh, wishing she'd run up the stairs when she'd had a chance. Mrs. Cantrell's son, Arthur, smiled at her as Yvette pretended to examine a small dog—a mutt to be exact—that was in perfect health.

"Isn't she clever, Arthur?" Mrs. Cantrell said, closely watching Yvette from a rocking chair.

Arthur scooted closer to Yvette until his upper arm pressed against hers. She stifled a groan. "He's fine," she said, placing Lancelot down.

"I just wanted to make sure." Mrs. Cantrell stood. "Let me go get you something to eat."

"No, that's okay," Yvette called after her, but Mrs. Cantrell had already disappeared into the kitchen.

Yvette briefly closed her eyes, determined not to move or say anything. She didn't want to hurt Arthur's feelings, but she did not want to encourage any advances.

"Mama's a really good cook," he said in a drawl Yvette wasn't sure was real.

"Yes, I know." She managed to move a couple of inches away from him.

Moments later Mrs. Cantrell returned with a

plate loaded with southern deep-fried chicken legs, greens and biscuits and handed it to Yvette. "Eat up. No man wants a skinny woman."

"This is really too much."

"You could never have too much." Mrs. Cantrell shoved a fork in her hand, and pulled up a collapsible tray resting nearby.

Reluctantly, Yvette took a bite, then made audible sounds of pleasure. Mrs. Cantrell smiled. Arthur did, too. But while the food was good, it was hard to enjoy a meal with two pairs of eyes watching. Yvette started to eat fast. "Thank you. This is delicious," she said, desperate to fill the silence.

Mrs. Cantrell returned to her rocking chair. "Did Arthur tell you he was promoted?"

Yvette shook her head and continued to eat as fast as she could.

Arthur rested his arm behind her head. "I'm now a regional manager."

Yvette swallowed before the food stuck in her throat. "That's great."

Mrs. Cantrell nodded. "And he got a salary increase."

"Mama," he said in protest.

"A woman likes to know these things." She smiled at Yvette, as though they were best friends. "Don't we?"

Yvette set her glass down on the side table, accidentally knocking over a picture of a man with a gun and a deer head. "That was wonderful."

Mrs. Cantrell rushed to her feet and stared at Yvette's plate. "You've hardly eaten anything."

Yvette stood, determined to reach the door before she did. "I had a large lunch."

"But—"

Yvette scooted toward the exit. "I really have to go." She dashed out the door and gulped in the fresh air of freedom. She raced up the stairs, but stopped when someone called out her name. She turned and saw Arthur.

"Could I talk to you for a minute?" He saw her hesitation and added, "I promise you it won't take long."

Yvette turned and started down the stairs, but stopped before she reached the bottom. "Okay, what is it?"

"I know you're not interested in me, but I was wondering if you could do me one favor. Then I promise you my mother will leave you alone."

She rested against the railing. "What is it?"

"My office is having a party this weekend and I'd like you to be my date." He waved his hands when she opened her mouth. "Before you say no, please hear me out. I know I'm not handsome or debonair. But I'm a good guy and I'd like to show the guys at my office that I'm not some lonely workaholic, that I can get a woman like you interested in me."

Yvette straightened. "Arthur, you're fine the way you are. You've just been promoted. You don't need to impress anyone. Besides I'm no one special."

He took a step toward her and clasped her hand in both of his. "Yes, you are, and it would really mean a lot to me. Please. Just one night."

Yvette stared at her trapped hand, then sighed. "Okay."

His face lit up. "Really?"

"Yes. I'll do it."

"Really?"

She pointed at him. "If you ask me that one more time, I'll change my mind."

"Right. I'll send you the date and time." He pulled her close and kissed her on the cheek, his lips as thick and meaty as the rest of him. "Thanks, Yvette. I'll make sure we have a great time."

She only nodded, trying not to wipe the wet residue of his kiss off her cheek, then headed up the stairs to her apartment. Once inside she turned on the stereo, fell onto her couch and picked up *On the Town,* an upscale magazine. She flipped through its pages, which showed the beautiful, rich and famous at play. Yvette loved looking through the magazine and had stacks of them and others like it, near her bed and on her coffee table. One of her favorite pastimes was allowing herself to imagine living like the people she saw in the pictures; eating sumptuous foods, wearing luxurious clothes and jewelry and traveling to exotic destinations.

This was her part-time hobby and she had learned a lot. Her apartment looked exactly like a room she had seen in *Architectural Digest,* and she had done it on her budget, by mixing and matching and finding incredible sales at local designer showrooms. Her wardrobe showed the same attention. Just like her furniture, Yvette knew where to find designer clothes at 50–70 percent discount, and loved selecting pieces that made her stand out.

It was nearly eight o'clock before Yvette realized that she hadn't checked her mail. She snuck down the stairs, relieved when she saw that Mrs. Cantrell's door was closed. She quickly collected her mail, then returned to her apartment, but before she opened the door her neighbor, Elliot Walker, an orthodontist, poked his head out. He was recently separated from his wife and desperate to catch Yvette's attention as he segued back into the dating world.

He smiled, his teeth perfectly straight and white as ivory. Unfortunately, everything else about him was crooked from his tie to his business practices. "Hey, Yvette."

"No."

"You say that every night."

"It's a hint, Elliot."

He stood in the doorway. "Dinner for one night. I'm a great cook. Or if you don't want to come over, we can go out."

"No."

"I know you're not seeing anyone. Come on."

Yvette opened her door and hurried inside. "Good night, Elliot." She closed her door, walked into her living room and flipped through her mail. Junk, junk, junk. A postcard from her parents, which made her smile. More junk. Then she saw it. An invitation crushed between a magazine subscription renewal and a sample for dryer sheets. Yvette stared at it, intrigued, then opened it.

It was a handwritten note, on expensive parchment paper, lined with finely woven lace in a gold envelope.

You have been personally selected to join The Black Stockings Society, an elite, members-only club that will change your life and help you find the man of your dreams. Guaranteed.

Guaranteed? Yvette didn't believe in guarantees. She studied the invitation wondering what they were trying to sell, but couldn't find anything. She continued to read.

Dumped? Bored? Tired of Being Single?

No. No. No. What a silly ad. She began to crumble it and throw it in her wastebasket, but the last question caught her eye.

Ready to live dangerously?

Now *that* was an interesting question. Her gaze fell on the magazine filled with people living exciting, fascinating lives. She would love to do that just for a while. Yes, she was ready to live dangerously. She sat and continued to read.

Then this is the club for you. Guaranteed Results! Submit your application today.

There was that word again, *guaranteed*. It was probably not true, but it had piqued her interest and she decided to go for it. There was no harm in trying. Yvette grabbed a pen then began filling out the enclosed questionnaire. Some of the questions didn't make sense to her. She skipped over them until she read a phrase at the bottom: *All questions must be answered as honestly as you can.* She sighed and reread the earlier ones:

What's the most important thing in the world to you? Respect.

Would you prefer diamonds or pearls?
Diamonds.

What would your ideal man be like? I don't
have one. Yvette groaned. Why does everyone
think you have to have an ideal man? She began
to skip the question, then remembered what
she had read earlier. She chewed her lip, carefully considering her answer. An ideal man?
She didn't have any idea. She thought of Elliot.
He was cute, but needy. Plus she didn't like that
he drove a luxury car although he worked at a
government-funded dentistry practice. Definitely
crooked. She could never be with a man like
that.

She thought about Arthur. He had a good job,
but his self-esteem was shaky and his relationship
with his mother was cause for concern. And then
there was Lewis, but she couldn't think of him as
an ideal anything. As for the other men she'd had
in her life—none of them had really impressed
her.

She buried her head in her hands. She couldn't
think of anyone. She pushed the questionnaire
aside and returned to her magazine. While
flipping through the pages she stopped at
the photo of a couple lounging on a boat in the
Mediterranean. Although they were partially in
shadow, something about the man reminded her

of Mrs. Kerner's nephew, Nate. If she could describe him in three words they would be— *confident, rich* and *mysterious*. Yes, she could deal with that. A man who would leave her alone, but listen to her when she wanted him to. A man with enough money to afford all of her wants, and yet a man with some mystery—to keep her interested. Yvette quickly wrote down the qualities, then nodded, satisfied.

After completing the form, Yvette read the "sworn oath" at the bottom of the page out loud: *As a member of The Black Stockings Society, I swear I will not reveal club secrets, I will accept nothing but the best and I will no longer settle for less.*

The next morning Yvette wrote a check for the nominal fee, dropped the application in the mail on her way to work and instantly forgot about it the moment she realized that James had been abandoned. Another day ended without a sign of Margaret. Yvette had trusted her to return and as a result she hadn't asked for too much personal information. Unfortunately, James was of no help. He didn't have any identifying tags or a microchip. On the third day, Yvette was anxious because she knew James was headed for the animal shelter.

"You know, he's kind of old," Greg, her assistant, said when she told him. "It may not be easy for him to get adopted."

Yvette attached a new leather leash to James's collar. He began furiously wagging his tail. "He'll find someone." She set him down.

Greg bent down to pet him. "Why don't you take him?"

"I don't have time for a dog."

He straightened. "What if the lady fell on hard times and comes back and realizes James is gone?"

"Or got hit by a bus or abducted by aliens? Things happen. That's life. That's why we have shelters. We can't keep him here indefinitely, and I can't take him."

"How about just for a week?"

"Why a week?"

Greg lifted James. "I may be able to convince my brother to take him, but it may take a while. I think that's better than the shelter, where we don't know what will happen to him. Look at this handsome boy. Don't you want to make sure he's taken care of?" James stared at her.

Yvette looked into the dog's soulful brown eyes and felt her resolve weakening. She turned away. "Fine. One week. Then he either goes to your brother or to the shelter."

Greg grinned in triumph. "Thanks." He turned

to James. "Give her a kiss." James licked her cheek. "See, he's smart."

Yvette wiped it away. "His days are still numbered."

The same day Yvette took James home, a small package arrived. When Yvette opened it, she found four pairs of stockings, a membership card that read: *Yvette Pamela Coulier, Member, The Black Stockings Society* and strict instructions. Yvette scoffed at them. For an offer that promised the recipient they would *live life dangerously* there seemed to be a lot of rules. But she decided to put her own bias aside.

Welcome to The Black Stockings Society. Your first assignment is to go to your favorite hair salon, where you need to dye your hair a soft black.

Black? Ordinary black? What kind of dangerous living was that? So far this "society" wasn't anything like she'd hoped. Yvette rushed into her bathroom and looked at herself. She loved her dramatic blond streaks. She hadn't worn her hair black in years. How did the club know the color of her hair? That wasn't one of the questions. She rested her hands on the sink and stared at her reflection. Perhaps a change was in order. A new, more conservative look may make people treat her differently. She made an appointment with her stylist for the next day. Unfortunately, she hardly slept that night. James snored. She tried burying her head under her two pillows, reminding herself that there were only six more days, but his snoring still penetrated her flimsy sound barrier. Luckily, she soon fell asleep out of exhaustion.

The next day at the salon when Yvette told Geena, her stylist, about coloring her hair black, she looked at Yvette as though she'd grown antennae. "Black? You want me to dye your hair just black?"

"Yes."

"Not purple or pink?"

"No."

"How about just a hint of orange?"

Yvette shook her head determined. "Nope. I'm trying for a more refined look and that starts with having my hair dyed a soft black."

Geena sighed. "All right. It's your hair."

Nearly two hours later, Yvette looked divine with a classic chic cut and black hair. Geena spun the chair around and looked at her, astounded. "The color actually suits you."

Yvette smiled. "Who knew the biggest change would be looking more like myself?"

Once back home, Yvette looked curiously at her next set of directions. *Wear the sheer control stockings to work.* Now that was strange. Hadn't these people read what she did for a living? How was she going to wear stocking while grooming a dog? Her normal work attire consisted of a pair of jeans (designer, of course) in the winter, and either shorts or capris in the spring and summer, with a blouse, sweater or jacket (in bold colors naturally) and funky footwear.

But she was determined to follow all the instructions, no matter what. The new hair color had worked. When she left Geena's, she couldn't help but notice that she was turning more heads than usual. The next morning, Yvette checked herself in the mirror. With her mid-calf cream jeans, bright designer sneakers, and yellow knee-high socks the stockings looked almost invisible. "At least I won't look too strange," she said, directing her conversation to James who sat quietly by her floor-length mirror. "Nobody's going to notice these."

But someone did notice, the moment he saw her.

Chapter 4

Nate hadn't expected to see anything interesting at Le Chic Hounds. But then again, few
things interested him. Most things bored him—
people, places, things. But the sight before him
wasn't boring at all. A beautiful woman, wearing
a rather colorful outfit and sheer stockings was
bent over a little dog and talking intently with its
owner. Lucky dog. When he closed the door
behind him, all eyes turned. He was used to
people staring. He was a Blackwell after all, and
that always warranted stares. But it was only
when he saw his reflection in a large wall mirror

that he realized the reason for their curious glances. He was wearing all black with a white poodle at the end of a diamond-encrusted leash. He suddenly realized that he had to remember that he was in Michigan not New York and people didn't know about him or his family connections.

"Can I help you?" a pretty woman with too much eye makeup said.

He gestured to the dog at his side. "Queen has an appointment."

"Of course. Yvette will help you."

The woman with the legs straightened, turned and smiled at him. And with each movement she became more and more interesting. He was transfixed. He could not remember the last time a woman had smiled at him without pretense. A brightness seemed to shine around her, and he no longer noticed the garish walls or the shelves of expensive products that lined them. Suddenly he had a feeling that he'd met her somewhere before, but couldn't place her. Then he noticed the earrings and remembered. This couldn't be the same woman.

"You've changed something," he said without thinking.

Yvette pulled out a strand of hair and playfully wiggled it. "I dyed my hair and cut it." She held out her hand to him. "I didn't introduce myself the last time we met. I'm Yvette and you must be Mr. Blackwell."

"Nate," he said surprised that her small delicate hand had such a strong grip.

Yvette suddenly looked uncomfortable. Nate saw her glance at the other woman. "Please follow me," she said and turned before he could argue. Not that he would. He knew being with her would never be boring and he enjoyed a very nice view of her backside and the way the light hit her legs made a man want to reach out and stroke them.

He followed her into the grooming area.

"I'm here for an appointment," he said when she continued to look uncomfortable.

"Yes, I know."

"But there's a problem?"

"Your appointment was yesterday."

Nate looked at her, stunned. "Are you serious?"

"Unfortunately, yes."

He swore and held his forehead. "She's going to kill me."

Yvette raised a brow. "Queen?"

"No, my sister." He pulled out his wallet. "I don't care how much extra it is, just tell me you'll take her today."

Yvette grinned and waved his wallet away. "These things happen. I'll take Queen if you have followed all of the drop-off instructions."

Nate pulled out a list his sister had given him. "You mean this?"

"Exactly."

"She hasn't eaten, she's done her morning, um…walk and…"

"That's fine." Yvette led Queen onto a steel surface then pressed a lever to lift it up.

"Nice."

"It certainly saves us having to lift big dogs. She's really medium size but I like to impress my clients."

"It's quiet around here. Are you the only one who works here?"

"No, it's a slow day today. Two of my assistants are out and the other has the day off."

"Are you sure you don't want a bonus?"

"Consider this a thank-you."

"For what?"

"The other day." Nate's expression looked blank so she said, "Your aunt." Yvette gently began to part Queen's fur. He shrugged. "That was nothing." Nate looked at her curious. "What are you doing?"

"Checking for any bumps, lumps or cuts on her skin."

"Oh." He came around the table, and stood closer to her.

Her voice rose in surprise. "What are you doing?"

"I just want to get a better view." His gaze met hers. Yvette's heartbeat picked up.

He maintained a respectable distance, but to Yvette it was too close. Her entire body felt on alert. Just when she was getting used to him being there he suddenly leaned forward, his chest touching her back, and pointed to something on Queen's skin. "What's that?"

Yvette swallowed, praying her voice would remain steady when she spoke. "It's nothing. She's had it since birth."

"Oh." He drew back, but not far enough. She could smell his cologne, and at times her arm would brush his jacket.

"Okay, that's done," she said, ready to send him on his way. Yvette lowered the scale and took Queen over to the large sink against the wall. "You can pick her up in a few hours or I can have her dropped at your house."

"Can I just wait? I like watching you."

"You do?"

He smiled. "I find this interesting."

Yvette hesitated, searching desperately for a reason to send him home. "I don't usually—"

"I promise I will not get in your way."

She began to shake her head. "I really don't…"

He pulled out some dollar bills. "I can pay for the privilege."

She frowned. "I wish you'd put that thing away."

"It's called a wallet and it has made life very easy for me."

"I bet."

"You don't sound as though you approve."

"It doesn't matter if I approve. What you're stating is a fact. Money means ease and special privilege."

"But it doesn't necessarily mean happiness."

"A tired cliché."

He leaned on the sink. "You don't believe it?"

"No. You may want to turn your face for this." She was happy for an excuse to create some distance between them.

He watched her put on a pair of latex gloves. "Why? What are you going to do?"

"Squeeze her anal sacs."

"Her what?"

Yvette lifted Queen's tail; Nate diverted his glance.

"Oh."

Yvette tried to remain professional, but all

she could think was that she had the chance to finally meet him again and here she was cleaning a dog's anus. Not very attractive. *Why did he have to stay? Why couldn't she make him leave?* Naturally, he looked every bit as handsome as she remembered. Even more so. His black jacket complemented his medium-brown skin and his unrelenting gaze hadn't changed. At their first meeting he'd been in a hurry, but he certainly wasn't in a hurry now.

"I'm surprised it doesn't smell like I thought it would," he said glancing around.

"How did you expect it to smell?"

"I expected it to stink, I guess."

She tightened her lips, offended. "A grooming salon should never stink. That's why we give our clients the drop-off rules. This ensures that when you bring your family member to us, they won't get sick or have a messy accident while in our care. At times, that still happens but rarely. The only smell there should be is that of a wet dog."

"I was just making an observation," he said by way of an apology.

"Now you know the reason."

He nodded. "I also know that I was right."

"About what?"

He turned to her, a hint of amusement in his eyes. "I told my sister you were smart."

Yvette looked away and turned on the faucet. "Thank you."

"But you're wrong about one thing. It's not a cliché that money doesn't buy happiness."

"Yes it is. You have to know how to be rich to be happy at it. People who are born into money take it for granted, but if I were given money I would cherish it every day and enjoy every penny."

Nate frowned as Yvette took off her gloves and tossed them in the wastebasket. "Do you have to do that with all of the dogs?"

"Some owners check the sacs themselves, but most request that we do it for them."

"What a job."

"Some people have to *earn* their money."

"I get the hint." Nate folded his arms and rested a shoulder against the wall. "Take it from me. Being wealthy isn't all it's cracked up to be."

"I think rich people only say that so others won't try to join them."

"It's true. There are the luxury business trips, the lavish parties and numerous wealthy and influential friends. But there are times when I just want to get away from it all. I thought I would get a chance this month, but then my sister scheduled two very important functions I'm supposed to attend with Queen and King."

"I'd love it. The parties, the socializing." Yvette began bathing Queen, feeling more relaxed.

"The endless chatter."

"The conversation."

Yvette finished shampooing and rinsed.

"The boredom."

"I could never be bored at a formal party or any high-society event!" She dried Queen with a towel, then led her to a large table to be blow-dried.

Nate stared at her in disbelief with a renewed interest. "You really mean it, don't you? You would like to go around socializing with two dogs?"

"I wouldn't want to be just a dog sitter, if that's what you mean," Yvette shouted over the sound of the dryer. "I've had enough of entering grand houses through the service quarters, thank you. For once in my life I would like to enter through the front door. Have someone address me by my name, rather than my job title. I want people to listen to my opinion because they think it's important, because I'm important."

Nate pushed himself from the wall. "I can make that happen."

"What?"

He pointed in the direction of the dryer. "I'll

wait until you're done." When Yvette had finished, he said, "I can make you rich." He rubbed his chin, thoughtful. "It will take some planning, but I'm sure we could pull it off. Actually I know we can. Are you in?"

"In what? I don't know what you're talking about." He was too close again, but Yvette couldn't move away.

"You want to be rich and I can make you rich. At least for a month. That's how long I'll be in town. I can introduce you to high-society people, get you invited to parties and you can take my place at the two functions my sister scheduled. I'll act as your valet."

"I thought only men had valets."

"No, women have assistants, too, if they have another name I don't care because a valet is the only thing I know how to imitate. No one here knows me so I can move around unnoticed." He clasped his hands together, satisfied. "This idea gets better and better."

"I don't think so." Yvette stared at him as though he had lost his senses.

"What are you afraid of?" He seized her shoulders, forcing her to face him. "We can make this work."

Yvette had never seen a man so animated. A part of her was drawn to it, but another part was still wary. "I don't even know you and it's a crazy idea."

"It's a great idea. Besides you know my aunt and my cousin and they will vouch for me. Although my aunt may not compliment my character, she has a certain bias." He shook his head. "It's probably better not to ask their opinion, they'll try to persuade you against it."

"Where would I live? Would I have to change my name? What about clothes and—"

Nate pounced on her interest, determined not to let her change her mind. "Leave that all to me and no, you wouldn't have to change your name. You will tell your family and friends that you've just come into a lot of money." He snapped his fingers. "I know. I'll give you a million dollar limit."

Yvette widened her eyes. "A million dollars!"

"I'll get you all the contacts you will need so that you are invited into the right circles. You said you wanted this and you'd be doing me a favor."

"Why me? You don't know what you're doing."

An irresistible grin spread across his face. "I always know what I'm doing." He winked. "Why not?" He lowered his voice to a persuasive whisper. "What do you say?"

Yvette remembered the invitation and the last question: *Are you ready to live dangerously?*

"Yes."

* * *

"You're right. It's crazy," Madlyn said as she, Lewis and Yvette closed for the day. Lewis had come by to take her out to dinner and she told them her plan, without mentioning how much Nate was willing to spend.

"I say it's perfect," Lewis said. "You could meet a rich man. Go for it."

Madlyn shook her head and leaned against the counter. "I think it's wrong."

"I already said yes," Yvette said, but they continued to argue.

"He'll pay for everything and she gets to be rich. What's wrong with that?"

"It's deceitful and Yvette may not be able to pull it off."

"You're just upset because she won't be around for an entire month."

Madlyn bristled at the implication. "That's not why."

"Or perhaps you're jealous."

"I'm not jealous. I have my own money. My question is what happens when the month is over. Will Cinderella turn back into a dog groomer?"

"Let's not think about the future," Lewis said. "Think of how much fun we'll have."

"We?" Yvette said.

"I mean you, but this arrangement will benefit all of us. You can use this opportunity to get Le Chic Hounds more name recognition. You could talk me up with new clients. This is something you've always wanted and he gets to take the break he wants. It's a win-win situation. Nothing could go wrong."

"He does have a point," Madlyn said, with some reluctance. "Perhaps with a little polish you could understand the clients we are trying to attract and you would be better able to handle them."

Yvette wanted to say "I'll never be a snob" but nodded instead.

"I do have one question," Madlyn said, looking at Yvette's crossed legs.

"What?"

"Where did you get those stockings? I couldn't help noticing."

Lewis laughed. "I'm sure others couldn't help noticing, either."

Yvette forced a smile, not knowing what to say. "Umm, there was a client who gave me a pair because she had extra."

"Who was the client?"

"I don't remember. I…just took them and tossed them in my drawer and rediscovered them this morning."

Madlyn nodded. "Lucky girl."

Lewis lifted an imaginary glass. "A toast to new beginnings."

"Yes," Yvette said. "And dreams coming true."

Chapter 5

Nate didn't believe in "happy ever afters" or "dreams coming true." Actually, he didn't believe in dreams at all, and he didn't have one that night. Instead the nightmare returned: the one that had been haunting him for years; this time more vicious and real than it had been in the past. He found himself in a room with no color and no exit.

Everything from the walls to the door to the windows was a blinding, cold, austere white and he couldn't escape. The white burned his eyes as he searched for a hint of color, crawling on his hands and knees looking for a crack in the walls or the floor, but found nothing. It wasn't heaven; it wasn't hell. It was a place of nothingness and it was turning him into nothing. Hollow and cold inside, slowly driving him insane.

Nate jumped up from his nightmare, startling the two canines who shared the room with him. He fumbled for the lamp, desperate for light although he was now awake, because he found no comfort in darkness. When he couldn't readily find the light, his movements became frantic. At last his fingers found the switch and light flooded the room. He welcomed the stinging glare of the bright light, his eyes eagerly drinking up the colors around him—the muted red walls, the wood furniture and impressionist paintings. He pushed the blankets away, his body trembling like a victim of aftershocks from an earthquake. He opened his bedroom window and took a deep breath, letting the cool early-morning air fill his lungs.

Nate returned to his bed and sat on the edge. Soon the trembling subsided, but the memory of the nightmare remained in his thoughts like an echo.

Queen jumped on the bed and began licking his face. The shock of her warm, wet tongue erased his morbid thoughts and he turned and patted her on the head. "Thanks. I needed that."

King jumped on the bed, too, and just stared at him. "Didn't mean to wake you." Nate ran a tired hand down his face. He couldn't risk returning to bed. He grabbed his robe and walked barefoot into the kitchen, the cool tiles a welcome comfort beneath his feet. Nate didn't cook, but knew how to heat up food, and Diana's chef, DeKay, had left plenty for him.

A few minutes later Nate sat at the dining table with a plate of stuffed eggplant and couscous. He didn't turn on the radio or TV. He was a man who'd grown used to solitude and treasured silence and being alone. After he finished his meal, he roamed the apartment. Bored, he grabbed his sketch pad, which he'd left lying nearby, and began sketching Queen as she lounged in front of the fireplace. Sketching had become a habit he'd developed over the last couple of years that no one knew about. He was careful to keep his efforts hidden.

After he'd sketched awhile, he tossed the pad aside and walked over to the enormous bay window in the living room and started to count the stars. He quickly grew bored and then tried counting the kitchen tiles, but sleep still remained elusive. He looked at the clock. It was three o'clock in the morning.

In a few days he'd be meeting with Yvette at

three. Three in the afternoon. The thought of her brought an unconscious smile to his face. Kim would have liked her. But the thought of Kim erased his smile. He hadn't come to Detroit to think about her, his father or his life back East. He was here not to think. For once in his life he didn't want to owe anyone anything, or be what someone needed him to be. And at last he was getting a chance to be ordinary, if only for four weeks.

Nate welcomed the change. For an entire month his life would be his own. While Yvette took center stage, he could disappear in the background. Instinctively he knew Yvette would fill the role well. She had the face for it. And the legs. God, what a pair of legs…and that figure. Too bad he hadn't met her a few years ago. They could have had fun. But he was a different man now. A man with secrets and a heartache that seemed to grow every day. But he was determined to still enjoy himself. He hoped Yvette liked wearing skirts. He would enjoy watching her in them. But he had decided early that it would definitely be a look—don't touch—relationship. He had too much to deal with already and he didn't want any messy entanglements. He'd had enough of those. But Yvette would be a nice diversion. A *very* nice diversion.

Nate lay back on the couch, keeping all the lights on, hoping pleasant thoughts would erase unpleasant ones, but the moment he slipped back into sleep the nightmare returned.

Yvette slept well that Friday night. It was the next day that proved to be a nightmare. It started with learning that James was allergic to her favorite perfume. He sneezed and sneezed until she was forced to bathe and remove the scent. Then, after going grocery shopping and doing some light housecleaning, she'd received a call from Arthur reminding her of their date. She'd forgotten and had to scramble out of her street clothes into something suitable.

"You are going to behave yourself," she told James. "If I come home and find one item damaged then you're going straight to the shelter no matter what Greg says."

James only looked at her, wagging his tail.

When the doorbell rang, Yvette pointed at him. "Be good." She opened the door. Arthur stood smiling at her and handed her a bouquet.

"You look great," he said.

When he stepped in, James growled. Arthur took a quick step back. "I didn't know you had a dog."

"It's temporary."

When Arthur made a move forward James's growl grew louder.

Yvette pointed at him. "Stop that."

"I'll just wait out here," Arthur said.

"Okay." Yvette put the bouquet in a vase then knelt in front of James. "I don't know what's wrong with you today, but I'll be okay." She stood and went to the door, but James raced in front of her and stood there.

"Don't try to make me feel guilty for leaving you."

He didn't move.

She bent down and patted him on the head. "I won't be gone long. I promise. I may even bring you back something special. Now move." She pointed to the couch. James stared at her, hung his head and then walked slowly over to the couch. She watched him, feeling guilty, and wondered if something could be wrong.

Arthur knocked on the door. "Are you almost done?"

"Yes, I'm coming." She took one last look at James then left.

The party was lively by the time they entered and there was a lot of ribbing as Arthur proudly showed off his date. After an hour of stares and being hit on by some of Arthur's coworkers, including his married boss, Yvette disappeared into

Arthur's office for some peace. She turned on the lights and stifled a scream. On the desk and all over his walls were framed pictures of her. One of the photos was from the tenant's barbecue last summer, another was a picture taken of her by Arthur as she sat on the doorstep and there were more.

"Yvette?"

She spun around. "What is all this?"

"It's not what you think," Arthur said in a nervous voice.

"Not what I think? People expected me. You've been lying."

"Look, we'd be perfect together. Do you see this view?" He pointed to the magnificent scenery that could be seen from his new corner office.

She walked past him. "Take me home."

"But the party—"

She raised a hand. "Is over."

When she returned to her apartment, James rushed up to greet her. "This is why I don't like men. I don't understand them but dogs I do. Going out with Arthur was a big mistake. I should have listened to you. Maybe Nate is a mistake, too." She picked up the phone, then put it down again. She'd given a total stranger her home number but to be fair, he had given her his and his cell phone. But she knew so little about him. She picked up the phone again and dialed. Nate picked up after two rings. "Hello?"

She froze.

"Yvette?"

"Yes, how did you know it was me?"

"I saw your number."

"Oh."

"Do you need something?"

"I need to ask you a few more questions."

"Okay."

"Are you single?"

"Yes."

"Are you looking for a girlfriend?"

"No."

"Do you have any hopes, plan or desire to get married any time soon?"

He laughed. "No."

"Good."

"What about you?"

"Me?" her voice cracked.

"Yes, do you have a boyfriend or want to get married soon?"

"No to both."

"So we're definitely in business. What triggered this phone call?"

She told him about her night with Arthur. He burst into laughter.

"I don't see the humor."

"That's okay. I do. The same thing happened to me once when I was sixteen except I didn't know the girl. She wanted to impress her mother so she cut out a picture of me she had found in one of those glitzy magazines and put it in her wallet. Then one day I visited the same restaurant she went to with her mother and when her mother saw me she rushed over and hugged me."

"What happened?"

"We dated a few months then broke up."

"You dated her?"

"Sure. It was fun and she was able to save face. But I made sure not to be in photos after that."

"You're a kind man."

"She was a good-looking woman. I wasn't being that kind."

Yvette argued with him for a while, then they talked about other dating disasters. He had more than she did. Before she knew it an hour had passed. "Sorry to have kept you so long."

"No problem. Now you know me enough to trust me. I'm not after you, so you're safe."

"Yes," Yvette said, wondering why she felt disappointed.

"I'll see you Tuesday."

Yvette hung up the phone, then smiled at

James. "I guess the night wasn't so bad after all." She looked at her calendar and saw she had an appointment with Rania, an etiquette consultant, on Monday after work. Yvette remembered her initial apprehension when she read the instructions from The Black Stockings Society that told her to contact Rania. She'd made the appointment with a brusque, but polite, woman who identified herself as Rania on the phone and now looked forward to meeting someone who was part of the Society. All Sunday she thought about her appointment and went to bed excited.

Unfortunately, her excitement fell when she saw the building. It was a brownstone. An ordinary brownstone with one skinny tree that had small yellow blossoms. Yvette checked the directions to make sure she was at the right address, hoping she'd made an error. But there hadn't been a mistake. She was at the right place. *She'd left work early for this?*

When she stepped inside, the interior didn't look much better than the exterior. Even her lower-priced apartment had a more engaging foyer. This one was as brown as mud with a frayed rug and pictures faded by the sun. Yvette looked at the directory and saw Right Touch Etiquette Services 205.

Yvette climbed the stairs, careful not to touch

the railing that looked ready to crumble into sawdust. Once she reached the second floor, she looked for suite 205 and sighed. The door had more grooves than a railway station. She'd expected something more elegant than this. She stuffed the instructions in her back jeans pocket, knocked then stepped into a lavishly furnished apartment.

"No!" a voice cried.

Yvette stumbled back, startled by the woman on the other side of the room. She was an attractive, dark-skinned, full-figured woman who would make the perfect headmistress in a boarding school with her fitted tweed suit, single-strand pearl necklace and expertly styled hair. "You've done it all wrong," she said. "Try again."

"Try what again?"

"Your entrance." She pointed to the door. "Walk into the room as though you were meant to be here."

"But—"

The woman continued to point to the door, her gesture as forceful as a shout.

Yvette raced out the door and closed it wondering if she should escape completely. Who was this mad woman? How was she supposed to make an entrance? Yvette gripped the door handle and took a deep breath. She was rarely intimidated and wouldn't be now. She could do this. After counting to three, she flung the door open then entered with her back straight and her head held high as though she were Madlyn.

"Excellent," the woman said. She stretched out her hand. "I'm Rania, your instructor." She glanced at Yvette's worn jeans. "Those will have to be thrown away immediately."

"You mean donated."

"No, I said what I meant." Rania made a circle around Yvette. "Presentation is important, but polishing you won't be too difficult. You have the right combination. I suppose we'll have to keep the earrings. I wouldn't want you to not be yourself, besides your hair covers them most of the time. Yes, you have everything you need."

"Huh?"

Rania paused. "*Huh* is not a word. It's a sound and no one wants to hear you making them."

"Sorry, I mean what did you say?"

"Don't worry about what I was saying. I was thinking aloud." Rania walked over to her desk, giving Yvette a chance to survey her surroundings. The apartment had been transformed. To one side lay a sumptuous dining area decorated like a faux restaurant, to the other an entertaining area. There was a photo area with a video camera, where Yvette could see that she was being taped. But it was the clothes closet that caught her attention. It resembled an upscale boutique, lined floor to ceiling with beautiful designs and shoes.

Rania noticed her look. "Yes, we'll start with clothing. Too many ladies wear inappropriate cocktail dresses to lunch meetings. It's better to be conservative than offensive, especially in international settings that have different cultural codes."

Rania spent the next two hours instructing Yvette on what to wear for different occasions, and was somewhat surprised at how quickly Yvette caught on. She then switched to the dining area.

"Dining with strangers is never just about eating. Do you want to seduce, impress, engage, instruct? All that will dictate how you behave. Good manners are all about the other person. Don't fake anything. Honesty is extremely attractive. It's better to say 'I don't know anything about wine' than to make the wrong selection.

"Don't lie to the waiters, but don't insult them. Be honest without being cruel. If they ask you if something is wrong with your meal and there is say, 'I wanted to try this meal, but didn't expect the hot pepper' or something similar to that. Always be gracious. Tip, even if the service isn't up to standard, and tip very well if you expect to return."

Rania set a bowl of soup in front of Yvette. "Begin."

Yvette lifted the spoon and started.

Rania gasped as though a spider had just fallen from the ceiling. "No, don't hunch over your food. You're not trying to write an essay for a history exam."

Yvette straightened.

"And don't open your mouth so wide, you should always sip from the side. Direct the spoon away from you as you ladle the soup, like a ship going out to sea. Yes, that's better. Good."

Rania instructed Yvette on how to butter bread, hold a wineglass and other table etiquette that had Yvette's mind spinning: "Never use toothpicks at the table. If you have something caught in your teeth, excuse yourself. Go directly to the ladies' room and remove it. Preferably, behind one of the stalls, you don't want anyone to see you. Don't freshen up your makeup or lipstick at the table, and never ever use your napkin as a tissue."

At the end of the session, Rania felt Yvette was ready. "So what is next on your schedule?" she asked.

Yvette told Rania the name of the restaurant where she was to meet Nate. The two of them spent another hour selecting an array of designer clothing that fit Yvette's slim form perfectly. She especially liked trying on the shoes, which were all in her size. She ended up with a complete new wardrobe. Rania watched Yvette, surprised. She had the eye. She knew quality. She knew what outfits and colors showed off her skin tone, eyes, hair color, and yes, her magnificent legs. Before she left Rania directed Yvette back to the closet and pulled out a simple gray dress. "You're going to wear this to your meeting with Nate."

Yvette thought her selection was horrible, but didn't voice her opinion. *She hated gray.* However, this was her chance to be gracious. "I've never worn anything like that. I don't think it will suit me."

"It will." She handed Yvette the dress. "Don't wear any jewelry, other than your watch, and put your hair up, to show off your neck. If you're concerned about anything, don't hesitate to call."

Resigned, Yvette went back to her apartment and hung the dress, along with the other items, in her closet. It was completely wrong for her. No loud colors, no daring curves. It looked perfect for someone who wanted to enter the nunnery.

She shoved the dress to the back of the closet then shut the door.

Yvette took James on his evening walk and got caught in an unexpected rainstorm. She returned to her building with a wet dog and soggy shoes. She'd gotten used to the snoring, and having to walk him in the morning and the evening and the cost of his food, but the rain fiasco only made her more determined to find him a new home.

Mrs. Cantrell came into the hallway as Yvette pulled off her soaked jacket. "You got caught in the rain."

"Yes," she said, resisting the urge to wring out her jacket in front of her.

"You should have had an umbrella."

"I know."

"Arthur always carries an umbrella with him," she said as Yvette headed up the stairs. "He likes to be prepared for anything."

"Uh-huh."

"He hasn't stopped talking about the office party. You really had an effect on him."

Yvette gave a weak smile, then continued up the stairs, shaking her head. *One date and I'll get my mother off your back,* he'd promised. Of course that had been a lie, too. The moment she opened her door she heard another door open. "No, Elliot."

"I wasn't going to ask you out," he said in a hurt tone.

"That's a nice surprise."

"I just wanted to let you know that some guy stopped by."

James pushed his way inside the apartment. Yvette didn't notice. "What did he look like?"

"Tall, black, good-looking."

"That's not very specific. You just described yourself."

"You think I'm good-looking?"

Yvette sighed. "So you didn't see him clearly?"

"No, he wasn't here long."

She opened her door wider. "Thank you."

"Is he your new boyfriend?"

"No." Yvette quickly went inside, changed out of her wet clothes then spent the next few minutes drying James as she tried to solve her mystery. Who had stopped by? Was it Nate? Did he want to see her? Why would he? Did he want to cancel their lunch date? Should she call him? He didn't leave a note so it couldn't have been important.

At that moment the phone rang.

Yvette scrambled to pick it up. "Hello?" she said, a little breathless.

"Hi, it's Nate."

A thrill of pleasure raced through her. Three words and her knees felt like jelly. She checked her forehead. Perhaps she was coming down with a cold. Or perhaps she was just happy to get their plan started. Or perhaps...

"Yvette?"

"Yes?"

"I thought the line went dead."

"No, sorry. I'm here. I just came back from a walk."

"I won't take up your time."

"Okay." She hoped she didn't sound disappointed.

"Just calling to confirm our lunch date tomorrow," he said.

"Yes, everything is on schedule."

"Great. See you then."

"Wait!" she cried before he could hang up.

"What?"

"Did you stop by my place today?"

"No. Why would I do that?"

Yes, why? What a stupid question. Of course he wouldn't stop by. Why would he need to see her? She sounded self-obsessed. "No reason. There was a mix-up. I just wanted to make sure." She tried to sound casual although her face felt on fire.

"Fine. See you tomorrow."

Yvette hung up the phone feeling like an idiot.

Lewis had probably stopped by, although that was rare. Who else could it be?

The phone rang again. It was Lewis.

"Did you stop by?" she asked him.

"Yes, I thought we could go out."

She squeezed her eyes shut. It was a simple, ordinary explanation. She felt stupid. "Thanks, but I've got to be well rested."

"Oh, yes, your lunch with Prince Charming."

"He's not my Prince Charming."

"I bet you want him to be."

"I'm hanging up now. Why are you calling?"

"I wanted to make sure you're following through with the plan."

"Why?"

"I want to see you happy."

Yvette tapped the phone. It wasn't like Lewis to show this much interest in her life. Then again her life had taken an interesting turn. She couldn't blame him for wanting to be part of it. "I'm seeing him tomorrow. He just called me to confirm, you know, like a six-month dentist appointment. There's nothing more."

"Sure," Lewis said, but didn't sound convinced.

The next day brought blue skies and warm weather. Yvette pulled out the gray dress and winced. She fell backwards on the bed. *I'm going to hate this.* She sat up and held up the dress. It was just one day. She could suffer through one day. She grumbled as she pulled on the dress, cursed as she pulled her hair up and moaned as she put on her second pair of stockings. Immediately her mood changed. The silk feel of the stockings felt like a second skin, and the seam down the back added instant sex appeal to her most important attribute, after her face. Yvette slipped on a pair of cream-colored suede high heels then looked in the mirror.

She had expected to see a conservative bore staring back at her, but instead she saw a refined sophisticated woman. The dress wasn't as simple as she'd thought. It was an A-line dress, which complimented her figure. Although she had a slender build she was curvy in some areas, and the style worked. She was surprised to discover that the particular shade of gray brought out the softness of her sensuous skin. She would never have selected the color or style, yet it was perfect. The first pair of stockings she wore felt like a dream, this one was heavenly. Perhaps Rania was right. She winked at James, who lay on the bed.

"Eat your heart out."

He wagged his tail.

Yvette arrived a few minutes late and saw

Nate standing outside the restaurant under the awning. She smiled as she approached, then saw his face, and her smile disappeared.

Chapter 6

He was a drinker. There was no other explanation for it. She knew all the signs: The red eyes that fought to stay open. The unshaven face. They entered the restaurant and he held the door open for her, but didn't say anything beyond a casual "hello" before speaking to the host. When they were seated he didn't compliment her dress or talk about the weather. He just sat and stared at the menu. This wasn't the same man she'd spent nearly an hour talking to on the phone. He'd become a stranger again.

Yvette unfolded her napkin neatly on her lap,

remembering all of Rania's advice. But it didn't matter. She should have known it was all too good to be true. What sensible man would come up with a scheme like this? What other vices did he have? He had probably been with a woman last night. They'd likely been at some high-society function, had too much to drink, ended up in bed together, and he'd just woken up remembering he had a late lunch date with her.

At least the restaurant made up for her sullen companion. A violist played softly as waiters rushed past carrying dishes that looked more artistic than fulfilling. One plate consisted of three large scallops wrapped in clover; another displayed five jumbo shrimps mounted on scalloped garlic potatoes wrapped in seaweed. She heard the tinkle of fine china and the hushed sounds of intelligent conversation. Or at least she imagined it to be intelligent, she didn't expect any "late child payment" arguments here. At last she was in a place where she longed to be.

"Would you like me to order for you or suggest something?"

Yvette stared at Nate, surprised. His voice hadn't changed. She'd expected it to be hoarse or perhaps soft. Didn't drinkers usually have headaches the next day? Her father had. "Excuse me?"

He continued to stare at the menu. "Would you

like me to place your order or suggest something?"

"How can you suggest something when you
don't know what I like to eat?"

"I'm trying to offer a subtle hint for you to tell
me."

"Oh." She frowned. For someone with a
hangover he was incredibly sharp, but she still
wouldn't trust him to order for her. "I'm sure I
can find something on my own."

Yvette glanced back at the menu. She made
an effort not to wince at the prices. She selected
the cheapest item on the menu, then snapped it
closed. "I know what I'm going to have."

"What?"

"Grilled jumbo shrimp and scallops in a red
wine sauce."

He furrowed his brows, confused, as he read
the description. "That's just an appetizer."

"I know."

He glanced up at her with an accusatory look.
"I hope you're not on a diet."

"I'm not."

"Do you have a strange aversion to people
seeing you eat?"

"No."

He returned his gaze to the menu. "Then order
something sensible."

"I thought I did."

"That appetizer is about the size of my pinkie. So unless your stomach is the size of a pea, I suggest you order something else."

Yvette squirmed uneasily in her chair, finding it annoying that she had to argue with a man who didn't even look at her. "I wish you wouldn't make a big deal out of this."

"Either you order something or I'll order for you."

"No."

"Why not?"

"Because I can't afford it," she said in a loud whisper.

People from two tables away glanced at her. She placed her napkin on the table, ready to leave. "Maybe we should go somewhere else."

He covered her hand with his. It was large and unexpectedly soft and had the surprising effect of forcing her to stay and calming her at the same time. "I'm paying," he said. "I'm sorry I didn't make that clear." He removed his hand and for a moment she was sorry he had.

Yvette sat still. A man with a hangover shouldn't be able to look so sexy. The quiet voice, the stubble on his chin and his half-open eyes, instead of making him look like a tramp, gave him a rough, dangerous look that only made him more attractive. She found herself relaxing and stared at his hand, which now rested on the table. "I wasn't sure."

Again his gaze fell to the menu. She never knew someone could find a menu so interesting. "I always pay," he said. "Next time just ask."

She again spread her napkin on her lap. "I thought since this was sort of like a business meeting…"

"Do you think I'd take you to an expensive restaurant and have you split the bill?"

She shrugged. "It's happened before."

Nate glanced up from his menu, intrigued. "Really?"

"Yes. His name was…" She shook her head. "Well, it doesn't matter what his name was. He asked me out and took me to this wonderful restaurant and ordered half the items on the menu, then said we should split the bill."

"You didn't, of course."

"I was young at the time."

"How much was it?"

"Fifty dollars."

"That's not much."

"It was to me. Twenty-five dollars for dinner?"

"Hmm…well, I won't be doing that. I'm here to please."

Yvette clapped her hands together in delight. "Good. That changes everything."

When the waiter came to the table and requested their orders, Yvette said, "I would like the orange chicken without the oregano, and the asparagus in a light olive oil instead of butter, and can you please make sure that my potato is baked, not mashed. And I would also like a seat on the veranda."

The waiter sent Nate a glance for confirmation. Yvette caught the look and frowned. "You don't need to ask his permission. If you can't fulfill my request then I don't need to be here." She removed her napkin and laid it on the table.

"No," the waiter said quickly. "I won't be a moment."

He began to turn.

"Aren't you forgetting something?"

He looked at her, unsure. "I don't know."

She nodded at Nate. "My friend hasn't ordered yet."

"Oh, yes. What would you like, sir?"

Nate flashed Yvette a look of amusement. "The same thing she's having."

Moments later they sat outside under a bamboo umbrella with the afternoon sun cascading around them. Yvette sighed and stared up at the sky.

"You give orders very well," Nate said.

"Thank you. When you work with animals

you realize the importance of being firm. They respect people who are in charge." She winked at him. "Plus I wanted to try out my new role."

"I bet you'll enjoy ordering me around. You've started off with the right attitude."

Yes, she'd definitely love to order him around. She would begin with having him remove his shirt, then his trousers, then his... She adjusted her position. What were they talking about again? Oh, yes, attitude. "Is that said with approval or censure?"

"What would you like it to be?"

"Approval." She waved her finger. "And I know what you're going to say. That the rich don't care what anyone else thinks."

Nate stretched out his leg and it brushed hers. She didn't move, neither did he. She took a deep breath, reminding herself that it was no big deal.

"You're wrong. People don't care only if they're heartless. The rich have feelings like other people." He smiled. "I hope you don't find that too shocking."

The smile should have softened his face, but it only drew more attention to his unkempt appearance. She set her drink down in a slow, careful motion. "About our agreement."

He looked at her with a steady gaze. "Yes?"

His leg brushed hers again, sending an electric current through her. This time she knew it wasn't an accident. That only made it more distracting.

"I think you're a really nice guy, but—"

Nate sat back and held up his hands. "Wait a minute. That sentence sounds too familiar. Are you breaking up with me? Did we start dating and I forgot?"

"It's not a break-up speech. It's more of a reconsideration."

He leaned forward and gave her his full attention. "You don't want to move forward with the plan?"

She tried to move her leg away, but somehow it only brought them closer. "I don't think this is going to work." She clumsily adjusted her knife and fork.

"Why not?"

She squirmed in her seat. "I thought you said you don't like to party."

"I don't." His shoe touched her ankle. She set down her utensils. "Stop that!"

"Stop what?"

"What you're doing under the table."

Nate feigned innocence. "I'm not doing anything."

"Then keep still!"

He rested his chin in his hands and watched her, amused. "Okay. What were you saying?"

"We were talking about your partying."

"I don't party."

"Then why were you up late last night?"

He froze. "What are you talking about?"

"Your eyes are red and you're not completely shaven."

Nate sat up and rubbed his chin. "Sorry about that. I'll take better care next time."

"It's almost four o'clock. I can't have a valet who drinks!"

He lowered his gaze, pulled his leg back and returned to his meal. "I never drink to excess."

"Only sometimes?" she challenged. Her father had been in denial, too.

"I *never* drink to excess," he repeated softly.

"Then why—"

He spoke softly, slowly. "As I said, it won't happen again and you can take me at my word." Before she could reply he said, "Now let's get to business."

"Is it allergies?"

"No. Now I think—"

"A cold?"

"No, now, Yvette—"

"It's not only your eyes. Your skin is pale as

though you've stayed indoors for days. I didn't notice that before. I hope you don't do drugs."

"No," he said through clenched teeth. "I don't do drugs."

"Then why—"

"Yvette," Nate said with growing impatience. "I said let's get down to business."

"This is business! If we're going to work together I need to know all your vices."

"I don't have any vices. I don't drink. I don't party late. I don't do drugs and I don't have allergies."

"Then why are your eyes red?"

"Because I couldn't sleep last night," he snapped.

Yvette lowered her voice. "You suffer from insomnia?"

He returned to his lunch.

Yvette stared at him in disbelief. "Nate, I asked you a question. Didn't you hear me?"

"Yes, I did."

"And you're not going to respond?"

"No."

"That's very rude."

"Yes. I can be very rude and stubborn and come up with stupid ideas. This being one of them." He set his fork down and looked at her. "You're right. This won't work. We're com-

pletely incompatible. So enjoy your lunch and
this will be the end of it." He lifted his fork again
and resumed eating his meal.

"Fine." But it wasn't fine. She didn't care
that she'd changed her mind, but it felt different that he had. It wasn't a stupid idea. Now that
he'd taken away a dream opportunity from her
she wanted it even more. This was her chance
to be rich. She didn't care if he drank, as long
as it was in private. He was upset, but she was
even more upset. He may be used to shutting
people out, but he wouldn't shut her out. "Nate,
it's not as though I'm trying to delve deep into
your personal life. I bet you don't even do
anything for fun except find unsuspecting
strangers and build their hopes up before
snatching it away from them. Does that make
you happy?" She paused. "Aren't you going to
say anything?"

"I don't interrupt monologues." He sent her a
sly glance. "Plus I'm not easily provoked."

Yvette took a deep breath, resisting the urge
to smash her plate over his head, but she doubted
that would ruffle his eerie self-control. She
counted to three. *Breathe.* She would have to
learn to deal with him. She'd dealt with finicky
dogs, fearful dogs and spoiled dogs. She could
handle any man. Threats wouldn't work, cer-

tainly not shouting, and probably not tears. That's when a realization struck her and his appearance made perfect sense. She felt ashamed that she'd misjudged him. "Oh."

"Oh what?"

"Now I understand."

"You understand what?"

"Why you don't want to tell me the truth. I think I already know what it is and for a man like you that would be embarrassing to reveal." She nodded, pleased with her conclusion, and continued her lunch.

Nate set his fork down and laced his fingers together. "Okay, tell me."

"No."

"If you tell me, I'll let you know if you're right or wrong."

"You'll probably lie."

"I won't lie."

"If I tell you, will you tell me the truth?"

"Yes."

"Okay." Yvette sat back and folded her arms. "I believe you're running away from something. You're on vacation, but you don't look relaxed. Whatever you're trying to get away from has followed you here. You suffered a major blow. Perhaps a heartbreak and last night you were crying."

Nate's hands fell to the table, rattling the dishes. "I was *what?*"

"Crying. That's why your eyes are so red."

"I wasn't crying. I've never cried over a woman in my life."

Yvette shrugged. "I knew you would deny it." She continued eating.

"I'm not denying anything."

"Then why are your eyes red?"

Nate covered his eyes and groaned. "My God you're a stubborn woman."

"Yes. Will you answer my question?"

"Do I have a choice?" he said, his tone resigned but filled with amusement.

"Well?"

He shook his head and leaned back. "And impatient."

"Nate."

"The last few days have been difficult." He released a weary sigh. "I have nightmares."

"That's nothing to be ashamed of."

"Nightmares are for children."

"Plenty of adults have nightmares."

"Hmm."

"What are they about?"

"Nothing."

"Nothing?"

"Yes, and that's all I'm going to tell you." He signaled the waiter. "Let's go for a walk."

Once Nate closed a topic there was no chance to reopen it. Yvette tried, but he cleverly redirected her and after a few unsuccessful attempts she stopped. They walked several blocks and Yvette had the chance to enjoy a part of town she'd never been to before. When Nate stopped in front of a window, he swore. "Is this how I look? Hell, no wonder—"

"Now that you've explained it, it's all right."

"You're very understanding. Kim would have…" He shook his head, ashamed. "I'm sorry. You won't see me like this again."

Yvette wondered who Kim was, what she meant to him and if she was the cause of his sleepless nights. She wanted to tell him that she was sorry she'd thought the worst of him and that she was grateful for this opportunity, but instead she focused on the activities down the street. She saw a woman who looked familiar in the distance. When she noticed the hat she was certain it was Margaret. "Wait, I know that woman." She pushed through the crowd. "Excuse me," she called as she drew closer to the woman.

The woman turned, saw her, then started to run.

"I don't believe this." Yvette took off her heels and chased after her, darting through the crush of people. At last she reached her and spun her around. It wasn't Margaret.

Yvette stepped back, embarrassed. "I'm sorry. I thought you were someone else."

"Then no wonder she's hiding from you," the woman said as she caught herself from falling over.

"I really am sorry," Yvette said, but the woman hurried away. She covered her face. "Damn." She looked down at her stockings and grimaced. They were torn with a hole over the right big toe.

Nate came up behind her. "What was that about?"

Her hands fell to her side. "I thought that lady was Margaret. James's owner. She left him with me at the shop to get groomed and never picked him up. I'm looking after him right now, but I have to give him away."

Nate gently led Yvette over to a bench nearby and they both sat. "Why don't you keep him?"

Yvette slipped her shoes back on. "I don't have the time. By tomorrow he'll either be adopted by Greg's brother or taken to the shelter. I've done my seven days commitment."

"You have other pets?"

"No."

"Hmm."

"Do you?"

He shook his head.

"Then you understand that animals take care and time, which I don't have. I'm too busy trying to be successful."

"Seems odd for a groomer not to have pets. It's like a chef who hates to cook."

"I don't take my work home with me."

"Why did you choose to be a groomer?"

"I like animals and discovered I had a knack. Dogs were my true friends growing up."

"You didn't have many friends as a child?"

"Hardly any." Yvette smiled without humor. "Not much has changed."

"Why? You look like the type who would have been one of the most popular girls in school."

She shook her head. "No, I was the most unpopular."

"Why?"

She hesitated. "I had a speech impediment. The kids made fun of me and soon I stopped talking completely. My parents put me in a special program where we would read to Cindy, a lovely golden retriever, and she didn't judge us and I soon gained my confidence."

"With animals, but not with people."

"Animals never intentionally hurt you."

"True." He watched the crowd, then said, "You must have worked very hard. I don't detect an impediment."

She sniffed. "Yes, but you haven't asked me to read anything aloud. That's still a struggle. Every time I do I hear the echo of kids laughing at me."

"I see." Nate pulled out a small brown book from inside his jacket pocket, flipped it open, then handed it to her. "Go ahead. Read to me."

Yvette took the book and looked at the words scribbled inside, intrigued. "You carry a book of poems with you?"

"It's full of poems, quotes and sayings. I write down anything I find interesting. It keeps me focused. My grandmother said words are good for the soul." He pointed to a poem. "Here, read this one."

She handed it back. "No."

He gently pushed it toward her. "If you mess up, you can blame my handwriting."

"I really don't think—"

"Go on."

Yvette began, her voice starting to constrict. She stumbled over a few words and stuttered on others. But when she looked at Nate's face his expression didn't change. She couldn't detect mockery or amusement. He just sat there, almost impersonal, and it helped because he didn't pretend that her reading was great or hint that it was horrible. He just listened and soon the words on the page were no longer her enemy and began to flow from her mouth.

"Read another one," he said when she stopped.

She made mistakes again, but not as many as her first attempt, and when he had her read a third poem there were no errors at all. She closed the book and handed it back to him.

Nate placed it back inside his pocket. "The third time was the best."

"I know."

"That's the power of confidence."

"Were you popular in school?" she asked, already sure of his response.

He leaned forward, rested his elbows on his knees and gazed at the distance. "I've always been popular."

"Oh," she said, again seeing the chasm between them. "Did you like being popular?"

"Yes, I did."

"But you don't anymore?"

He turned to her. "It just doesn't matter to me as much," he said in a tired voice.

"Have you ever tried reading poetry before you sleep?"

Nate's jaw twitched and his gaze grew hard, but his tone, although soft, was filled with anguish. "I've tried everything."

Yvette gripped his hands, a bold move that surprised them both, but he didn't pull away. "You must keep trying. I struggled for years with my speech. One pathologist thought I would never improve, but I did. One day you will sleep and the nightmares will be gone." She said the words with such passion that it seemed to ignite a fire between them.

"My God," Nate said with wonder. "You understand." He pulled her close and kissed her. His mouth covered hers, not as a man who'd been offered hope, but one with a fierce desire, as though he wanted to claim her passion as his own. He kissed her, unafraid of stoking the fire between them that threatened to turn into a blaze.

Yvette trembled under the delicious assault. His lips, like him, had the sting of danger but felt very real. She could no longer deny how he affected her. When he finally drew away she could have sworn the world had started spinning faster.

"I wonder if I'm going to regret this," he said.

"Kissing me?"

A brilliant genuine smile spread on his face, lifting her heart. She wished he smiled more. "No. I don't regret that. You're an extraordinary woman. Beautiful, talented, courageous, but…" He bit his lip. "I hope I'm doing the right thing." He stood up and began to walk.

She hurried after him. "What do you mean?"

"Money changes people."

"Don't worry. I won't change."

He spun around and cupped her face in his hands. "Make me that promise," he said with an intensity that frightened her. "Promise me that our plan won't change you."

"I won't change," she promised, unsure of why he needed her to.

He kissed her again, this time with a hunger that almost made her crumble. He drew back and whispered, "I should stop kissing you."

"I don't mind," she said, trying to be nonchalant. "I mean it's just a friendly kiss."

The corner of his mouth kicked up in humor. "If you think that then I'm not very good."

"No, that's not what I meant."

His hands fell to his sides. "I know, but we can't move forward without being honest. There's no chance of us being an item. We have a month and then I will return to the east coast and my life there. A life that is drastically different than yours."

"Yes, and I will go back to my previous life."

"Do you still want to do this?"

"Do I get to keep the money I don't spend?"

He nodded. "Yes."

Yvette thought for a moment. But not for

long. She may never see him again, but she had the chance to finally live the life she wanted and knew she would have the money that would maintain it. She'd dreamed of what she would do with a million dollars many times. There was no turning back. She extended her hand out to Nate, as though he were already her valet. "Definitely."

He bent down and kissed it. "Then I am at your service."

Chapter 7

Three days later Greg looked at Yvette help-lessly. "My brother can't take him."

Yvette glanced down at James, who had his eye on a docile rottweiler in one of the cages. She'd taken care of everything. Her apartment was secure. Mrs. Cantrell had promised to water her plants. Her mail had been redirected, and she had given Greg all the instructions on how to run the store in her absence and now she had to take care of one minor problem: James.

"I've already had him for two extra days."

"I tried."

"Then I guess it's the shelter."

"You mean you can't keep him?"

"No, I'm about to embark on a wonderful journey and there's only room for one. No dogs allowed."

Greg shook his head, disappointed. "You two make a great pair."

"And he'll make someone else very happy." She patted Greg on the arm, ready to leave. "Now you're in charge. Good luck."

"You, too."

But luck wasn't on her side that day. At the Delores Fry Animal Shelter they told her they didn't have room. She drove an hour and a half to another location, but a moment after she entered the overcrowded waiting room filled with an assortment of dogs and cats and their disgruntled owners, who shouted or cried at the frazzled clerk, Yvette and James returned to her car.

"Okay," she said as she drove away. "I guess I'm stuck with you for a little while longer." She glanced at him and thought she detected a canine smirk. "We will find you a new home soon. Unfortunately, that has to wait. I have a date with destiny."

The Golchester Apartments were not hard to spot. They were a large stately structure near the heart of the city down on the water with a guard at the gate. She'd been to the residence before to groom a bichon frise. The guard smiled as she passed him. Inside the building, Yvette struggled with her luggage, a bouquet of now-wilted flowers and James on a leash. When she reached 2641 she used her elbow to ring the doorbell.

Nate opened the door. When he saw her, his face turned to fury. "What the hell is going on?"

Yvette squeezed past him, trying not to trip over King and Queen who came up to greet her and James. "I know I told you I wouldn't have James, but things became complicated."

He took her bags. "I'm not talking about the dog. I mean someone should have helped you with your luggage."

"I didn't see anyone when I took the elevator."

He paused. "Which elevator did you take?"

"The one around back close to the parking lot. I've taken it before."

He pinched the bridge of his nose. "Was it really large?"

"Yes."

He sighed. "That's the delivery entrance. You're supposed to go to the one in front."

"Oh."

"I'll have to show you later."

She shoved the flowers into his chest. "Here."

"What are these for?"

"I thought it would be nice to brighten up the place and…" her words died away as she caught a glimpse of the apartment. The lush exotic plants that decorated the living room made her bouquet look like weeds.

"I'll find a place to put these." He made a sweeping gesture with his hand. "Do you like it?"

"No," she said in a flat tone.

He nearly dropped the bouquet. "What?"

"It's too wonderful to like." She glanced up at the crystal chandelier that resembled a burst of fireworks, looked at the African game rug which complemented the Zuni baskets and the array of sculptures and fine artwork, probably originals, that graced the walls. She pointed to a room off to the side. "Will I be sleeping in there?"

He nodded.

"Well, it's just too big and gorgeous." She left the living room and went into the kitchen. "Too well equipped." Yvette could hardly contain her excitement. Each room looked like a page out of *On the Town* magazine. She walked past the dining area to the living room and then stood in front of one of the large windows. "The view is too expansive." She turned to him and winked. "I don't know how I will endure staying here for four entire weeks." She sunk into a couch. "But I will try my best not to complain."

Nate wouldn't complain, either. He was going to have a lot of fun looking after Yvette. He was already enjoying her tight jeans and fitted shirt and he could never get over her smile. He would make sure to keep her very happy this month. But he knew he'd have to remind himself to keep his hands off her. His mouth, too. He had no regrets. At that moment when she made him believe his nightmares would end he couldn't help himself.

He had behaved at the restaurant, at least he'd tried. He'd kept his gaze off her instead of secretly undressing her like he wanted to. Okay, he probably shouldn't have played with her under the table, but it was a chance he didn't want to pass up. He thought a walk would have helped. It should have.

Then she went chasing after a woman, bravely read poetry although he knew she felt awkward, then touched him and spoke to him as though she knew his struggle—as if she'd been with him during the sleepless nights—and something in him just opened up. It hadn't closed since. He watched her as she sat on the couch with her arms out, head back and eyes closed.

He grabbed his keys. "I have to run an errand. If you need anything you have my number."

"Don't worry about me." She waved him away. "I don't plan to move from this spot for the next hour."

Cathleen Kerner didn't get phone calls. So it came as a surprise when her housekeeper, Juanita, came into the living room where she sat with her mother and made that announcement.

When she handed Cathleen the phone, her mother stayed close by, making it clear that she planned to eavesdrop.

"Hello, this is Cathleen," she said, tentative in case the caller had made a mistake.

"Hi, this is Lewis. The photographer. I was at your house last week."

Cathleen gripped the phone, her breathing growing shallow. He didn't need to remind her of who he was. She already had a picture engraved in her mind. His handsome face grew prominent. "Yes, I remember you."

"The pictures are done."

"Okay."

"I'd like to show them to you."

She glanced at her mother, then squeaked, "To me?"

"Yes, would you be interested?"

Cathleen swallowed; she could feel her mother moving closer. Soon she'd be close enough to sit on her lap. "That would be nice."

"I think you'll be pleased. Perhaps we could go for coffee afterward."

"Okay." She rolled her eyes. *Why couldn't she think of anything else to say besides okay?*

"See you at four tomorrow?"

"Yes."

"I look forward to it." He gave her directions to a café not far from where she lived, then hung up.

Cathleen pushed the receiver button, then set it aside. He wanted to show her the pictures and take her out? She couldn't believe it.

"Well?" Penny demanded. "What was that about?"

Her mother's harsh voice brought her back to reality. Cathleen took a deep steadying breath, but her words still came out in a rush. "That was the photographer. The pictures are ready. I just have to go pick them up."

"The photographer called *you?* What do you know about photography? He must have made a mistake. Those artistic types are never organized. I'll pick them up."

"Mother, please. I really don't mind. Your schedule is so busy."

"It's not that busy. You're staying here and I'll pick them up. When will they be ready?"

Cathleen licked her lips. "Wednesday." Her lie nearly choked her. She'd never lied to her mother

before and if she found out, Cathleen knew she'd
be very angry. It was Friday; her mother was
always busy on the weekends with her friends.
Perhaps she could come up with a good excuse
later. Or maybe her mother would forget about the
pictures completely. No, she wouldn't. She'd
remember on Wednesday and be angry. The
thought of her mother's anger nearly forced her to
tell the truth, but she was already getting ready to
leave.

"Wednesday is fine. I'll straighten him out
when I get there."

The moment her mother was out of the room,
Cathleen jumped up and began to pace. Guilt
and relief were at war within her.

"What are you doing?" a familiar voice asked.

She spun around, saw Nate and her mood
lifted. Any time he came by she never felt alone.
She rushed forward and threw her arms around
him. "I'm so glad you're here."

He gave her a kiss and tenderly patted her
back. "What's wrong?"

She drew away. "I just lied to my mother," she
said as though confessing a crime.

"So what?"

"It wasn't for a worthy cause or anything big."

"What was the reason?"

She lowered her gaze.

He lifted her chin. "You know you can tell me."

"So I could see a man," she whispered.

"Good for you."

She frowned, certain he was making fun of her. "This is serious."

"I know." He sat and sank into the couch. "What's his name?"

"Lewis." She sat down beside him, nervously pressing her hands between her knees. "He's a photographer. You might remember him. He came to take the pictures of Binky."

"Yes, I do remember." Nate clicked his tongue in sympathy. "Aunty would never approve."

Cathleen wrung her hands. "I know. Perhaps I should tell her—"

Nate straightened. "No, you won't tell her anything." He rested a brotherly arm around her. "Go out. Have fun. You're a grown woman."

"But I don't know if I can do this."

"Sure you can."

She kept her gaze on her lap. "I've never been on a date before. I've never been out on my own with a man. Although it's not really a date, it's going to sort of feel like a date, even if it's just coffee. I don't know why he would want to have coffee with me." She looked up at Nate in panic. "What should I say or do?"

Nate gently squeezed her. "You'll be fine. Be

yourself. That's the person he wants to see." He kissed her on the forehead. "I approve. He obviously has excellent taste."

"Thank you. You always make me feel better." Cathleen hugged him tight. Tighter than she needed to.

Nate pulled away. "Don't."

She brushed away tears. "Sorry, I can't help it. When I think about last year. It was so horrible."

"Then don't think about it."

"It's not that easy. I don't know how you can be so apathetic about it."

He glanced toward the patio. "I don't have a choice."

"Still don't want to talk about it?"

He stood, his voice harsh. "I never want to talk about it."

She looked up at him. "But it still bothers you. You're still not sleeping. I can tell. What did the doctor say?"

"What she always says."

"Will you—"

He rested his hands on his hips. "I didn't come to talk about me."

"Why did you come?"

He scratched his head. "I have to ask your mother a favor."

Cathleen bit her lip. "Oh, dear."

"I'm optimistic." He held his hand out to her.

She took it and he lifted her to her feet. "Why?"

"Because you're going to help me."

"What do you want me to do?"

"I need to convince her to do something."

Cathleen laughed. "Convince my mother? That will take a miracle."

"Perhaps, but first let me tell you what I'm up to."

"Absolutely not," Penny said. She stared at her nephew as though he'd just asked her to walk naked down the street. "Introduce some dog groomer to my friends?"

They sat in the sunroom where a crystal pitcher of iced tea, bite-size sandwiches and pastries were displayed on the table. "She only does that as a hobby," Nate said. "She's come into some money and needs the right connections."

"Well, they won't be my mine."

Nate took one of Binky's paws. "I see they're not as tender as before. You took her advice."

Penny stroked Binky's coat.

Cathleen reached over to touch Binky, but her mother slapped her hand away. Cathleen rubbed her hand. "She seems happier."

"Nobody asked you." Penny looked at Nate.

"The girl knows dogs. I'll give her that. But that's all. I don't care how much money she has come into, there's a difference between being rich and being wealthy and it's called class."

Nate took a sip of his iced tea and cringed. "Where's the sugar?"

"Sugar is a Southern thing. That's why they're all fat down there; they put sugar in everything. Drink it natural."

Nate pushed his glass away, wisely not glancing at her plump figure or reminding her of their Southern ancestors. "Now about Yvette—"

"No."

"What was the name of your first husband? Didn't his father slaughter hogs or something?"

His aunt sent him a warning look. "Nathaniel."

Cathleen shook her head. "No, they were turkeys."

Penny stared at her daughter, outraged. "Cathleen!"

Nate tapped the side of his glass. "I guess that means you're just rich."

Penny pursed her lips, then became resigned under Nate's intense stare. "Ellen is holding a get-together. I suppose it wouldn't hurt if that girl attended."

"Her name is Yvette and you will refer to her as Yvette."

She made an impatient gesture with her hand. "Very well."

"I know you two will get on."

"We'll see," she said, doubtful.

Nate's tone hardened. "I know you two will get on."

Penny nodded, hearing the warning in his tone. "Yes, we will."

"Good." He stood and kissed her cheek.

She brushed him away. "Your father called me."

He shrugged.

"He wants to know if you've come to a decision."

"He'll get it when I have one."

"He told me Kim also—"

Nate glanced at his watch. "Damn, I'm going to be late. See you later." He dashed out of the room.

Cathleen followed him to the front door. "Why are you doing this for Yvette?"

"It's a little experiment."

"Some experiments tend to blow up."

"Maybe, but I'm willing to take the risk."

"Is that the only risk you're willing to take?"

He paused. "Yes, for now."

True to her word, when Nate returned to the apartment Yvette was sitting in the same position he'd left her. Except her legs were up and she was resting her head on a large velvet pillow.

"Sorry I'm late," he teased. "Hope you're still enduring."

"I am. Where were you?"

"I was speaking to Cathleen. She has a date."

Yvette sat up. "A date?"

He nodded. "Surprised me, too."

"What's his name?"

"Lewis. The guy you were with." Nate shoved his hands in his pockets. "You don't look pleased. Hoping to keep him for yourself?" he said in an odd tone.

Yvette chose her words carefully not wanting to say anything bad about his cousin. "No, it's just that Cathleen doesn't seem his type."

He sent her a significant look. "Types change."

"Not with Lewis." She shrugged. "Maybe he's growing up. Cathleen seems really nice."

"She is and Lewis may help her come out of her shell. She's desperate for attention and needs to get away from the control of her mother. She's already starting to show signs of independence."

"I guess." She paused. "It's just—"

"They're adults. Don't interfere."

Yvette looked pensive.

"Yvette," he warned.

"I won't."

He sat beside her. "I have some good news. You have an appointment next weekend. My aunt has extended an invitation to you to attend her weekly social group."

"Your *aunt?* Are you crazy? Only a week ago I was trimming the toenails of her dog."

"That's all forgotten. This will be a great proving ground. If you can survive her friends you can survive anything."

"Where will you be?"

"Doing my best to stay out of view. You'll be fine."

Yvette was fine the first week she got to be a millionaire. She stunned Nate by first establishing a fund at the shelter for homeless people to come in once a year to get free care for their dogs and to provide some form of help for the owners. She also invested in a company she'd overheard one of her clients raving about and put money into Le Chic Hound for newer equipment and more advertising. Madlyn was so thankful she could have kissed her.

Yvette's spending habits amazed Nate. He had expected her to go out and buy a fancy car (she said hers worked fine), clothes and jewelry (she said she'd do that later) and visit all the top restaurants and high-society hot spots. Instead her first big purchase was for him.

"That's for me?" he asked, staring at the large black chair.

"Yes, it's an insomniac's dream." She pushed him into the chair. "It folds into a bed, but first let me show you this." She handed him a helmet with a visor and placed it on his head. A beach image appeared and he heard seagulls. "They promise that it will relax you and send you to sleep. What do you think?"

He thought she was sweet and didn't want to tell her that he had two at home. "This is great, but you shouldn't have gone—"

"It's no problem."

He lifted an extra helmet. "You should try it, too."

"No, I—"

He pulled her down next to him and placed her helmet on.

"We're on a beach," she said, fascinated.

"And you're wearing a bikini."

"No, I'm not."

"This is my virtual reality."

"Then you're wearing—" she stopped.

"What?"

She waved her hand. "Nothing."

He smiled. "Even better."

"That's not what I meant."

"Too late, you already said it. Ah, I see it now…oops your bikini top just fell off."

"Nate."

"It's okay, you don't mind. I don't mind, either. Now for the bottoms…"

She changed the scene. "Now we're in the mountains."

"In a nice log cabin with a large rug and a roaring fire." With a touch of a button he made the fire brighter and changed the shape of the rug. "And nothing to do but—"

Yvette removed her helmet and stared at him. "You've done this before."

He reluctantly nodded. "Yes, I'm sorry."

She stood, disappointed. "I should have known I couldn't get you anything special."

"I appreciate it, but I don't want you to think about me. It's time for you to have fun."

And that is exactly what Yvette did. She took a helicopter ride over the city, traveled to Montreal to visit her parents and sister and treated them to a live show. She went to an exclusive spa and indulged in almost every treatment, but as the weekend approached her worries began to build. How would she handle Mrs. Kerner's friends? What would she say?

"Everything will be all right," Nate said on the drive there. "You have nothing to worry about."

Chapter 8

Yvette didn't know what to expect when she entered the grand residence of Ellen Levigne, but Yvette certainly looked like a wealthy heiress. Her hair was pulled back and held in place with two emerald hairpins. She wore a knee-length yellow print dress that showed off her figure and her magnificent legs. As she glanced around, the antiques and hardwood flooring came as no surprise, but what did was the awkward figure standing near the wall.

"Cathleen," Yvette said with relief. "I didn't know you'd be here."

"I always come. It's nice to see you again." Cathleen looked at Nate and started to laugh. "What are you wearing?"

He tugged on the lapels of his jacket. "I'm supposed to be a valet."

"You look like a chauffer."

"Today I am."

"Get rid of the hat." She reached for it.

He moved away. "I like the hat."

"Get rid of it anyway. Tell him, Yvette."

Yvette shook her head. "I've tried. He won't listen."

Nate looked around. "Where is everyone?"

"They're outside. I came inside to greet you."

"Any trouble?"

"Not yet. Mom hasn't mentioned anything about Yvette yet."

"That's good."

They fell silent, then Cathleen cleared her throat. "I'd like to speak to Yvette alone."

"Okay. I'll go find something to do."

"Go flirt with the kitchen staff, that always keeps the butler busy."

Nate shook his head, then left. Cathleen looped her arm through Yvette's as though she wanted to share something private, but when she didn't speak Yvette said, "Lewis told me the pictures were ready. Did you see them?"

An Important Message from the Publisher

Dear Reader,

Because you've chosen to read one of our fine novels, I'd like to say "thank you"! And, as a special way to say thank you, I'm offering to send you two more Kimani Romance novels and two surprise gifts – absolutely FREE! These books will keep it real with true-to-life African American characters that turn up the heat and sizzle with passion.

Please enjoy the free books and gifts with our compliments...

Linda Gill

Publisher, Kimani Press

Peel off Seal and Place Inside...

Two NEW Kimani Romance™ Novels
Two exciting surprise gifts

YES! I have placed my Editor's "thank you" Free Gifts seal in the space provided at right. Please send me 2 FREE books, and my 2 FREE Mystery Gifts. I understand that I am under no obligation to purchase anything further, as explained on the back of this card.

PLACE
FREE GIFTS
SEAL
HERE

DETACH AND MAIL CARD TODAY!

168 XDL ERR5   368 XDL ERSH

FIRST NAME

LAST NAME

ADDRESS

APT.#

CITY

STATE/PROV.

ZIP/POSTAL CODE

Thank You!

(K-ROM-08)

The Reader Service — Here's How It Works:

Cathleen blushed. "They were wonderful. Lewis is very talented. You're very talented, too," she quickly added.

Yvette brushed the compliment aside. "That's okay. I don't need my ego stroked."

"He's also very smart. We talked for nearly two hours." She glanced around, then lowered her voice. "I had to explain to mother that I'd gotten the dates wrong and then gotten lost. I'd never lied to her so much in my life. I also saw him again this week."

Penny's voice rang clear in their direction. "Come, Yvette, we can't have Cathleen monopolizing your time."

"How did she know I was here?" Yvette asked.

Nate passed them carrying the newspaper and a drink. "Because she can smell fear."

Cathleen playfully hit him. "Ignore him. She probably heard our footsteps."

"We're waiting!" she called.

Yvette gripped Cathleen's arm. "To the firing squad."

Cathleen patted her hand. "You'll be fine." They both walked toward the women gathered on the patio. The group was smaller than she'd feared. Besides Penny, there were only two other women. One had a long chin oddly balanced by an equally long forehead and the other wore a fitted paisley dress that emphasized a slim physique that defied any evidence of her fifty plus years.

As Yvette drew closer, she could overhear their conversation. Penny's voice rose above the rest. "Only two weeks ago she was a dog groomer and then came into money."

"Astounding," Long Chin said.

Paisley Dress frowned. "So suddenly?"

Penny nodded. "Yes, some relative left her money. I'm looking after her. I knew she was meant for a better life when I first met her. She owns part of Le Chic Hounds, just as a hobby of course. She likes to make sure all aspects of her business are taken care of. That's the only reason she would ever groom a dog herself." Penny saw Yvette and smiled. "Ah, and here she is." She made introductions—Long Chin was Regina Matthews and Paisley Dress was the host, Ellen Levigne—then they fell into chitchat but a few seconds later a small woman carrying a little dog rushed in and sat down breathless. "Have you said anything interesting?" she asked.

"No," Regina said. "Not yet. We have a visitor."

The small woman grinned at Yvette. "I'm Estelle Walters."

"Yvette Coulier."

"Always nice to see a new face. I knew that there was someone new because I saw a strange man in the corridor. He was sitting reading a newspaper and when he saw me he actually winked. Is he yours?"

Yvette hesitated, unsure what she meant by the statement. "He's my valet, yes."

Ellen nodded. "Excellent choice, my dear. I saw him myself. He's absolutely delicious."

The three women nodded.

Yvette fiddled with the napkin on her lap suddenly uncomfortable. "Yes, but he's just my valet."

"Of course," Regina said. "I have one myself. I call him my personal assistant."

Estelle shrugged. "Assistants are nice. I prefer gardeners." A sly grin touched her mouth. "They know the *lay* of the land and like to tend to details."

Ellen shook her head. "Nothing beats a personal chef in my opinion. Good in the kitchen and good in bed. That's all I need."

Penny hastily spread cheese on a cracker and began eating. "Yvette is sensible like me. When she wants a man she'll marry him like I did."

"Yes, Penny, you can marry a man, but that doesn't prevent you from playing with boys." Her face spread into a knowing smile. "And if you have one nearby, playtime is easy."

Cathleen leaned forward. "What kind of play?"

"Drink your tea," Penny insisted.

Ellen turned to Yvette. "Call him."

Yvette paused, stunned. "Call him?"

"Yes, your man. Tell him that you need something. I want to check him out. I can always tell what fun you can have with a man, or boy for that matter, by just looking at him."

Yvette began to stand. "Okay, I'll get him."

"Sit down," Penny said. "We have people for that."

Ellen rang a bell and her housekeeper appeared. "Tell the young man in the corridor that Ms. Coulier wishes to see him."

Yvette looked at the group, panicked. "But I don't need him. What am I supposed to say?"

"You'll think of something."

Unfortunately, by the time Nate appeared she still hadn't come up with a reason to call him. He stopped at the table. "Yes?"

When Penny saw him she nearly jumped out of her seat. "What are you—"

He stopped her with a look. "Is there a problem?" he asked in a smooth, neutral voice. "I'm here to serve Ms. Coulier that's all." He looked at Yvette. "What did you need, madam?"

Yvette searched for a reason. "I wanted the chef to know that I don't want any spices on my food." The housekeeper arrived with a tray of glasses and more iced tea.

"I already spoke to her. I also made sure that your iced tea is sweetened." He sent Penny a look. "Some people can afford the extra calories."

Penny snatched her drink.

Yvette smiled. "Thank you."

"Is that all?"

"Yes."

Ellen pressed the tips of her fingers together. "Do you mind if I borrow him for a moment?"

Yvette blinked. "No."

She smiled at Nate. "Could you get me that shawl over there?" She pointed to a shawl draped over a lounge chair near the pool.

"Of course." He walked away and the women watched him—for different reasons. Penny frowned, Estelle grinned, Regina looked curious and Ellen looked like a cat eyeing a canary on the edge of a dish of milk.

"Excellent form," she said.

Penny picked up another cracker. "I don't think we should have this conversation. He could overhear us."

"So what?" Regina said. "Then he might show off for us."

Estelle stroked her dog. "Is it wrong to hope that he'll trip and fall into the pool?"

Regina began to giggle. "Yes, he'd look even better wet."

"So what do you think he's good for?" Yvette asked.

Ellen turned to her and winked. "Everything."

They burst into laughter.

"Quiet," Penny said. "He's coming back."

The women quickly sobered. Nate returned and draped the shawl on Ellen's shoulders, lightly touching her skin.

Ellen rested her hand on his. "Thank you, young man."

"Speaking of young men," Regina said. "How is that nephew of yours, Penny? What is he up to now?"

Penny sent Nate a stern glance. "I'm not sure."

"Will you ever let us see a picture of him?"

"He shies away from pictures. My poor brother only has ten or so pictures of him. I believe most of them were taken when he was under the age of twelve."

Ellen shook her head. "It's always hard to pin down a troublemaker, but they're also so interesting. Has Kim been able to—"

Penny cast another glance at Nate, then an accusatory one at Cathleen. "I think it's best not to talk about him today."

"But we always do."

"I'd really rather not." Penny glanced around desperate for a change in topic, then noticed Estelle's dog. "Yvette knows a lot about dogs, Estelle."

Estelle's face brightened. "Really? That's wonderful." She lifted her dog. "What do you think of Lucy's new ribbons?"

Yvette forced a smile. The poor little dog seemed to be drowning in them. It had a ribbon around both ears and three down its tail. "They suit her."

"Perfect color," Nate said.

"You can leave now," Penny said.

"No, let him stay," Ellen insisted. "He can sit by me." She looked at Yvette. "Do you mind?"

Yvette shook her head and looked at Nate, who didn't seem surprised at all. He was used to drawing attention. "No, that's fine." Nate sat down close to her. She made sure his thighs touched hers.

Estelle adjusted one of Lucy's ribbons. "She's a teacup poodle. I don't mean to brag, but she was very expensive."

Yvette hoped not. One look at the dog and she doubted Estelle had a teacup poodle. First, Lucy was too large in both weight and height and Yvette doubted she was pure bred because her nose was long, when it should have been short.

"Where did you get him?" she asked.

"Through Marshall Post. It's by appointment only to see pups at his shop. I actually got Lucy at a deal. He's wonderful."

"I see." *Most scam artists were,* Yvette thought, certain that this Mr. Post had swindled the trusting woman.

Cathleen joined in. "I've always wanted my own dog. Perhaps—"

"You don't need a dog," Penny said. "You have Binky."

Yvette was eager to meet this man. "I might want a new dog myself. How can I meet him?"

Estelle shook her head. "It won't be that easy. As I said, he has to invite you."

"Is there a way you could make an introduction?"

"He'll be at the Care for Animals charity at the end of the month. Will you be there?"

Yvette glanced at Nate. "I'll have to check my schedule."

He nodded. "Yes, you'll be there."

Estelle clapped her hands. "Great. I'll introduce you then, but I can't guarantee an invitation to him right away. It took me a while."

Yvette smiled with confidence. "If he's a man, an introduction will be all I need."

*   *   *

"You're not happy," Nate said, staring at Yvette in the rearview mirror as he drove her home.

She glanced up. "Why do you say that?"

"It's not like you to be quiet. What's wrong with Estelle's dog?"

"How did you guess?"

"I saw the expression on your face when she told you the breed and you seemed very eager to meet the seller. Don't worry, no one else suspected. I've just gotten to know you. So what's wrong?"

"I think she was scammed. Lucy is definitely not a teacup poodle and if she spent what I think she did, she was ripped off. Lucy's a mutt that was sold at a pure-bred price. It is a very lucrative business for bogus puppy breeders to sell dogs with false documents. I want to find out who this man is."

"What will you do if you find him?"

"I'll think of something. I'll track him down and expose him."

"That could be dangerous."

"I won't get into any trouble."

Nate shook his head, unconvinced.

"Besides, I'll have you there to protect me." She frowned. "Then again you've probably never been in a fight before."

"I have."

She blinked surprised. "What were the stakes? A woman?"

"Life and death."

Her voice cracked. "Oh."

"I obviously won," he said in a dry tone.

"Glad to hear it."

He met her gaze in the mirror. "So I'd be able to protect you."

Yvette lowered her gaze, feeling both scared and safe at the same time. Yes, she could imagine him being vicious. She stared at his hands as they gripped the steering wheel, she could see him wrapping them around someone's neck. She'd seen him upset, but she'd never seen him angry and she didn't want to. She liked him too much and had never felt this comfortable with anyone except her family. "Pull over."

"Why?"

"Because I want to sit next to you."

"You don't sit next to the chauffer."

"And the chauffer isn't supposed to argue with his employer."

Nate sighed and pulled over to the side, allowing Yvette to climb into the front seat. "Stop frowning," she told him as she buckled her seatbelt.

He checked the traffic, then merged. "I still think it's a bad idea."

"What's wrong with sitting in the front seat?"

"I'm talking about going after Mr. Post."

"I'll just ask a few key questions then I'll call the authorities."

"You probably won't have time anyway."

"What do you mean?"

"Get ready for invites to a number of upcoming events. Those ladies really liked you."

"So?" She tapped his hat forward. "They liked you, too."

He pushed his hat back. "I figured that."

"Cathleen's right. The hat is silly." She pulled it off.

He snatched it back and put it on. "I don't care."

"Your Aunt was surprised to see you there. Why didn't you tell her about us?"

"She wouldn't have approved. I had to catch her off guard."

"Well, you certainly succeeded."

"I know, but my aunt isn't the topic. We've entered the next stage of our plan. You're in. I hope you're up for all that's going to happen."

"I'm up for anything."

"Good." He grinned. "Because we're going to Paris."

Chapter 9

Yvette had been to Paris once before to visit a great aunt but she'd never seen Paris in a luxury car driving along *La plus belle avenue du monde,* otherwise known as the Champs Élysées, and she hadn't stayed in a private apartment in an exclusive hotel with a view of the Eiffel Tower. King, Queen and James had been left in a very posh pet hotel back in the States, but naturally it didn't compare to her hotel. Prior to their business arrangement, Nate had already booked a brief visit to Paris.

The hotel guest suites consisted of two luxurious private chambers, furnished with a collection of eclectic furniture that provided elegance and functional diversity. In Yvette's room was an elegant canopy bed with silk bedding and curtains, polished stone nightstand tops and twenty-four-carat gold-leaf lamps and an enormous private bath and sauna. Nate's room was just as extravagant with mostly white furniture, but it was the art collection throughout the suite that made her breathless. Original paintings, on loan to the hotel, consisted of pieces by Louise Mailou Jones and Matisse. The main living area had two settees crafted in France with an Indian motif and fitted with cushions covered in silk. The two marble tables, with ebony stone carved lamps featured semiprecious-stone-inlaid tops, and led out to a private terrace.

She turned to Nate, who had just closed the door behind the porter. "How did you manage all this?"

"That is not the question you're supposed to ask me."

"What am I supposed to ask you?"

"What's for dinner?"

"I don't think I can eat."

Someone knocked on the door. "You will," Nate said, then opened the door to a chef and his crew.

Yvette did eat that evening. Very well. They

were served a five-course meal consisting of braised lamb, steamed lobster and vegetables, a collection of just-baked French bread and a full tray of French pastries. Nate refused to eat with her because that wasn't part of his job so she sat at the table alone while he sat on the couch.

"I can see why people travel to Paris for their honeymoons," she said.

"Or affairs."

"Yes, that, too." She stared at him. "How many have you had?"

"Of what?"

"Affairs."

"In Paris?"

"Have there been many?"

He began to smile.

She rolled her eyes. "You're not going to tell me, are you?"

"It's best that I don't."

"That many? I'm not surprised. Is that why we're here? So you can resume your affair with someone?"

He sent her a devious look. "Perhaps I plan to start one."

She felt her skin grow warm. "What's stopping you?"

He stood and walked over to the table. "My conscience."

"What's it telling you?" Yvette challenged.

Nate held up an apple from the fruit bowl and studied it as Adam would have the forbidden fruit. "To stay away." He gave her a knowing look.

"Do you think you can?" she asked, boldly walking into dangerous territory. She saw a glimpse of his smoldering eyes determined to explore its depths.

He set the apple down. "I've resisted temptation before."

She held his gaze and came from around the table, closing the barrier between them. "Why resist?"

He didn't move away, but didn't move closer. "Because it's the right thing to do."

"What about what *feels* right?" She sat on the table and crossed her legs, letting her skirt inch up her thigh.

His gaze fell to her legs and a sly grin curved his mouth. "You don't know me very well, Yvette."

"In case you haven't noticed I'm trying to change that." She slowly lifted the skirt higher and could feel the tension in him grow. The heat of his gaze nearly scorched her.

His hand came down over hers in a swift motion. His large palm pressed against her hand

and thigh. She licked her lips, determined not to tremble from his touch. His eyes captured hers. "I'm not part of the package," he said in a quiet tone.

Yvette snapped back as though he'd struck her and yanked her hand free. "What?"

He softly swore then sighed with regret. "I didn't mean it like that."

She jumped off the table. "Then why did you say it?"

He lifted her back on it. "Because I don't want to mess this up. This is too important to me. You're too important to me."

"I don't understand."

"If I were to sleep with you there would be no turning back. Do you think I could be an impartial valet? I would want to break the fingers of any man who touched you, gouge out the eyes of any man who gazed at you for too long. I'm a possessive man, Yvette, and when I claim a woman she's mine."

"Fine." She jumped down again.

Nate gripped her waist and he set her back on the table. "Listen to me. I need distance. I need this space. So much of my life has been people wanting more and more of me and...if the circumstances had been different we wouldn't be talking right now." He grabbed her shoulders. "It's better for both of us to keep this as business-like as we can. If you must think of me, think of me as the wind that caresses your cheek." His thumb gently touched the side of her face. Her heart quickened. "The breeze that lingers on your lips and brushes your skin but cannot hold you." She could feel his breath on her face and longed for their lips to meet. "You can think of all these things, but you cannot think of me." He turned away.

"Even if my heart breaks?" she said in French.

He spun around confused. "What?"

She didn't care if he didn't understand her. That made her feel more daring. She leaped from the table and gathered the front of his shirt in her fist and pulled him toward her. "You arrogant buffoon. How can you compare yourself to things I cannot hold when you are standing here solid and real?" She rested a hand on his chest, wishing she could melt the fabric of his shirt away. "I want you in my arms and I want you in my bed."

Nate shook his head, frustrated. "Yvette, I don't—"

"I don't care if you don't understand me. This is the only language you need to understand." She kissed his neck, inhaling the intoxicating scent of his skin, which felt warm beneath her lips. She touched it with the tip of her tongue, wishing she could devour him. "I know you want me," she whispered, arching her hips against the evidence of his passion. "Why make both of us suffer?" She wrapped one arm around his neck. "You can touch me if you want," she said, but when he didn't move she realized she'd said the words in French and repeated them in English. He still didn't move, but his dark eyes challenged her to continue.

She took up the challenge. She spoke in French again and lifted his hands. "You might need instructions. Your hands are large and probably clumsy so let me help you." She tugged on her shirt. *"Chemisier."* She unbuttoned it and showed her bra. *"Brassière."* She unlatched her bra. *"Sein."* She rested his hand on her chest and began to smile, wondering if he would snatch his hand away. But to her surprise he didn't. Instead he pushed her bra aside and cupped her breast then tapped his mouth with his other hand, an indication that he wanted to know the word for it.

"La bouche," she choked, no longer feeling in control as she had been.

A deviiish look entered his eyes then he lowered his mouth and covered her nipple. She gasped but before she could recover, his mouth moved to her other breast and then her mouth.

"Let me torment you a little," he said in a low growl against her lips.

He could torment her all night. She wrapped her arms around him. His hands slid down the back of her skirt and cupped her bottom, pressing her closer to him.

She sank her hand into his pocket and moved toward the bulge in his pants. "Careful, Yvette."

But Yvette didn't hear him as her fingers touched small round objects filling his pocket. She pulled one out, curious. "What's this?"

He swore and took it from her, his tone brusque, his mood changing just as abruptly. "It's nothing."

She stared at him concerned. "Is it to help you with your insomnia?"

"Yes," he grumbled, stuffing his shirt back in his trousers. He glanced at her then latched her bra and buttoned her blouse proving his hands weren't clumsy at all. Unfortunately for Yvette they were engaged in the wrong activity. Nate stepped away from her. "What I said about us stands. It's a bad idea." He pressed a finger to her lips, his intense gaze holding hers. "You'll have to trust me."

Yvette nodded then sadly watched him go to his room.

No matter what he said she couldn't stop

thinking about him. No matter how he tried to keep his distance he was more visible to her than he was before. When he helped her with her coat and his fingers lightly brushed her neck, the area felt warm for hours. She noticed his hands, his legs, his mouth and wanted them to be somewhere near her. Everything about him proved to be fascinating. She knew his footsteps, the cadence of his voice and no other sound pleased her more. But Nate tried his best to keep her occupied no doubt for her sake and for his.

He planned her schedule and made sure it was full. She had a front-row seat at David Anton's couture fashion show, which was a grand performance where the clothing received the applause. He had also arranged for her to go Elle Elements, a highly admired local boutique.

Selections at Elle Elements consisted of unique and one-of-a-kind clothing. From her years of studying high fashion Yvette knew that the right clothing attracts and reflects glamour, money and beauty. She was shrewd with her money, but did splurge on several pieces. Nate went shopping with her but never gave his opinion although his was the only one she wanted to hear. After shopping, Nate whisked Yvette off to parties, dinner at some of Paris's best restaurants and live shows. She enjoyed every moment and four days flew by like a dream.

As she sat alone in the hotel restaurant she wished that a photographer was there to take her picture so she could capture the moment. She looked stunning and knew it. She loved her off-the-shoulder, white couture pantsuit with sequined floral embroidery around the neck, and offset by a pair of gold rhinestone-studded center-strap shoes with clear acrylic heels. She wore her hair pulled back and twisted into a roll, with two large mother-of-pearl hairpins. Delicately fashioned twenty-four-carat gold earrings finished the look.

The restaurant was as elaborately furnished as their suite and provided tables with drapes for privacy if requested by a guest. At last *she* was one of those women in the magazines, but those women were rarely pictured eating alone: they had someone with them and she only wanted one man to be by her side.

Her dissatisfaction made her feel guilty. Nate had proven to be an expert valet. All her needs were tended to. Although, there were times he looked tired from his sleepless nights. On one occasion when he'd cut himself in the kitchen. He told her he was clumsy with knives after she'd asked him about the spots of blood on the napkins in the wastebasket. He probably hadn't been paying attention due to lack of sleep. Yet he never complained. She could do anything. Attend any event, go to any shop, but more times than not she found herself wanting to be somewhere with him.

Yvette wished she could be with the man she had talked to on the phone about dating disasters, or the man she'd read poetry to. But after their first night in Paris Nate was all business, and yet how he treated others surprised her. Like the time when she saw him give up his seat to an older gentleman, and when he gave money for flowers and told the patron to give them to the next lady who entered the store. And there was the time he flirted with a baker whose day had started off badly due to a city-wide power outage. If only he would pay that kind of attention to her. How she craved that special look again just once and to be in his arms and to have his mouth cover hers…

"You're not by yourself I hope," a male voice said above her. "Such beauty cannot be so carelessly neglected. It's like the perfect grape being left to wither on the vine."

She glanced up and saw a large gentleman, just as attractive as his voice, and though his words were saccharine, his gaze was bittersweet as if he were trying to be happy in a world that had already disappointed him. She gestured to one of the empty chairs.

Although he spoke to her in English she replied in French. "Poet or painter?"

He sat, pleased, and spoke in French, as well. "Both. How did you guess?"

She pointed to a small blue paint stain marring the smooth brown surface of his hand.

He removed his hands from the table. "I apologize. I was in a rush this morning."

"I'm Yvette Coulier."

"I'm Bernard Leroy."

"Really?"

His brows shot up. "You've heard of me?"

She shook her head in regret. "No, but maybe I will one day."

"Perhaps."

"You don't sound convinced."

He tapped the side of his head. "The gray hair reminds me of the years passing."

"You're not that old. About forty-five?"

His eyes twinkled. "I'm thirty-five."

She tried not to show too much surprise. "Oh."

"You don't believe me."

"I do," she said quickly, embarrassed that her guess was off by ten years.

"Years of indulgence. But I'm not here to tell you my life story. I want to ask you a favor."

Yvette leaned forward, intrigued. "What?"

"I want to paint you."

"Really?"

"You doubt my sincerity?"

"No," Yvette said, afraid she might have insulted him. "I've just never been asked."

"Well, now you have. I'm asking. May I paint you?"

A voice, clearly not Yvette's, responded to his request with a quick, firm "No."

They both glanced up and saw Nate. Yvette smiled; Bernard froze. Nate pulled out a chair, sat and rested his arms on the table. He looked at Yvette. "Is that clear?"

Her smile grew.

He frowned, then looked at Bernard who seemed to have recovered from his shock. "She's not doing nudity."

"I didn't say anything about nudity."

Nate measured him with a look. "I'm sure you would like to see her without her clothes on."

"I'm certain I'm not the only one," he softly replied.

Yvette waved her hand between them. "Excuse me gentlemen, but I'm still here." This time she spoke in English.

Nate ignored her and responded in French. "When a woman is naked in my room she isn't sitting still. I—"

Bernard winced and lifted his hands. "Enough! Your French is awful. Let us speak in English."

"No, I want to practice," Nate said, continuing to speak in French.

"Must you practice so badly?" Bernard said in English.

"Only until I improve."

Bernard covered his ears. "I am in pain. You speak and your words are like daggers."

"Good."

Yvette saw Bernard's face and glanced around, not wanting to draw any more attention. "Nate, I really think you're hurting him. Please stop."

He turned to her. "Do you think my French is bad?"

"Yes."

The two men looked at each other then burst into laughter.

"Beautiful and honest," Bernard said. He patted Nate on the back, but was soon on his feet giving Nate a warm greeting, as if they were long lost friends. There were more hugs and kisses on the cheek and a quick conversation that Yvette couldn't follow, then they were back in their seats again.

She stared at the pair, confused. "You two know each other? What's so funny?"

Bernard looked at Yvette. "You cannot trust this man. He is not what he seems."

"Yvette knows most of my tricks," Nate said in perfect French.

"But not all of them," she said, cautious. He was a master of disguise. One moment he was the rich playboy, then the valet, and now a bohemian traveler fluent in French.

"So what are you two doing here?" Bernard asked.

"Holiday." Nate glanced at his watch.

Yvette noticed the motion. "Do we have to be somewhere?"

Bernard shook his head. "You Americans are always chasing what you already have—time. Sit awhile."

They did and Bernard entertained them with stories. Three hours passed before they finally decided to leave.

"I would really like to paint you both," Bernard said. "I see you two and the picture is now complete."

Nate began to shake his head, but Yvette responded before he could say anything, "We'd be delighted. But we're getting ready to go back to the U.S. in a couple of days."

Bernard handed Yvette his card. "Tomorrow." He nodded to Nate. "You know where it is," he said, then left.

"He's wonderful," Yvette said.

"And very smart."

"What do you mean?"

"You know it's a clever ploy."

"Ploy?"

"He frequents expensive hotels, charms rich women and offers to paint their portrait. Naturally they pay him for the privilege."

She thought of Ellen's idea of men as playthings. "I wonder if that's the only privilege."

"He's not your type."

"I don't have a type." She stroked her chin, pretending to be thoughtful. "A woman could get bored."

Nate sent her a stern look. "I'll make sure you're not bored."

"Yes, but it's not every day that a woman has a chance to have an affair in Paris."

Nate stood. "Are you ready to go?"

Yvette slowly rose to her feet then froze as a realization struck her. "You speak French," she said, her cheeks burning as she remembered the daring words she had said that night.

He grinned, amusement in his eyes. "Yes."

She could feel her skin grow hot. "Fluently."

"Yes," he said again, then leaned toward her and whispered in her ear. "And I remember a few words you taught me. Would you like me to repeat them?"

She swallowed and stared him, wary. "No."

He ignored her and traced his finger along the top of her blouse. *"Chemisier."* He lowered his finger to reveal the top of her bra. *"Brassière."* He touched the curve of her breast. *"Sein."* He winked. "Am I right?"

She pushed his hand away, feeling as if her entire body was on fire, her heart hammering in her chest. She wanted him to look at her like this, but not out in public. "Let's go."

"Are you sure you're ready?"

"I'm ready for something." She bent down, lightly touching her bottom to the front of his trousers. She swayed back and forth as she pretended to adjust the strap of her shoe. When she finally felt the affect she wanted, she stood and smiled, pleased that her teasing had worked. "I'm just curious how long I have to wait." She glanced down, resisting the urge to grab him in her hand. She spun away. "Shouldn't be too long."

"So how much does she know?" Bernard asked as he and Nate sat in a small hidden café the next morning. He loved the sounds of people going back and forth, and the smells coming out of the shops.

Nate sighed. "Nothing."

"Why not? She's bound to find out."

Nate lifted his mug. "Not if no one tells her."

Bernard sat back in his chair and muttered something.

"That didn't sound like French."

"That's because I like to swear in English. You're making a mistake."

Nate shook his head. "It's not what you think. We're playing a little game. It will end soon and then we'll go our separate ways."

"But you like her."

"I've liked plenty of women."

"But not like this. I see how you look at her, but more important, I see how she looks at you."

Nate picked up his croissant. "I can't help that."

"Why do you hesitate? A man should not heat up an oven and not put a cake in it."

"You just made that up."

"One day I'll be old. I want to start sounding wise."

"You're not there yet."

"But you get my meaning. She is a beautiful, desirable woman who obviously wants you. Do not deny yourself this tasty treat."

Nate held up his hand as though fending off the idea. "No more relationships for me."

"Why?"

"You know why."

"How do you f—"

He shot him a cold look. "I've told you never to ask me that."

"I'm sorry."

"So now you understand."

"But it still doesn't make the reason clear."

Nate shrugged.

"So you've given up? That's your decision?"

He shrugged again.

"I'm sorry to hear that." Bernard sighed fiercely, but not one to stay annoyed long, he winked at a passing waitress, smiled at an old man walking by, then changed the subject. "How is the little leaf?"

Nate couldn't help a smile. Bernard had given Cathleen that nickname because she always trembled when her mother was around. "She's fine."

"Is her mother—" He made a helpless gesture with his hand searching for words.

"Yes."

"Poor thing."

"Perhaps not. She's finally caught the interest of someone."

Bernard nearly choked on his coffee. "She's seeing a man?"

"Yes."

Bernard nodded. "Perhaps there's hope in the world after all. I'll see you later."

"This portrait better be quick."

"Of course."

"Are you almost finished?" Nate demanded, his booming voice startling the pigeons that had decided to rest on the windowsill.

"Keep still," Bernard ordered.

"You've taken our picture a million times and sketched us for over an hour."

"Less."

"Don't rush him," Yvette said.

Nate sighed. He stood behind her holding a tray of red grapes and a glass of wine while wearing a valet uniform. Yvette lay on a velvet red couch, directly in front of him, adorned in a sensuous sky-blue evening gown. "You say that because you're more comfortable."

"Don't ruin this for me," Yvette said. "Only a few weeks ago I was preparing a dog for a moment like this and now I'm the focus of the attention. I want to enjoy it."

"You're doing an excellent job."

"Feed her a grape," Bernard said.

Nate stiffened. "What?"

"Sit on the couch with her and feed her a grape."

Nate ripped a grape from the bunch.

"Be careful," Bernard cried. "I don't want them bruised."

Nate softly swore, then bent toward Yvette and pressed the cool grape against her bottom lip.

"Put it in a little farther. Yes. Stop. That's perfect."

Her lips touched his fingers. Yvette looked into his eyes, her heart constricting at the dark compelling pools that watched her. What thoughts did he have? Did he think that with one small gesture his fingers would be in her mouth? Did he remember their kiss? Did he ever wonder what it would feel like to kiss her again? She dropped her gaze, desperate to focus on something else and noticed how wide his shoulders were and how his fitted white shirt emphasized the muscles beneath it.

"I'm finished."

They didn't move. Nate's gaze dropped from her eyes to her lips. "Do you want to eat it?"

She nodded.

He released the grape and she closed her mouth, but not before closing her lips over his fingers. He slowly pulled them away. "Was it good?"

She nodded again.

He flashed an enigmatic smile and stood.

Yvette allowed herself to breathe.

Nate walked over to Bernard, who stood behind his canvas.

"Stay where you are," Bernard said.

Nate stopped. "Don't be dramatic."

"Drama makes life more interesting. No one sees my work until it is finished."

"When will that be?"

Bernard looked at Yvette then Nate. "In three weeks."

"That's too long," Yvette said. "We won't—" She stopped before she said *be together.*

Nate folded his arms. "And we can't spend any more time in Paris." Cathleen had called to let him know that she had gone out two more times with Lewis and felt she was falling in love. When he told Yvette she was concerned, but he told her not to be.

Bernard put his pencil down. "It will be worth the wait. Don't worry, I'll ship it to you. At your expense of course." He smiled. "You can afford it."

Chapter 10

Yvette wasn't sure what woke her that night, but the sound of movement outside her door got her out of bed. She grabbed her satin robe, pulled it over her pink boudoir set and left the bedroom.

The apartment was dark and for a moment she thought the sound had been in her dream, but then she heard the sounds of the city and saw the balcony door open. She walked over to it and found Nate sitting at the table, sketching. In the distance the Eiffel Tower shone and the scents of Paris—the wet streets, the diesel fumes, the shops and flowers that laced the balcony—

surrounded them. She walked up behind him and saw a charcoal sketch of the street below.

"That's very good," she said.

He leaped up and spun around. She backed away. She no longer had to imagine what his chest looked like. He only wore a pair of jeans. She'd seen him in a suit, she'd seen him in a chauffeur's uniform, and even in a shirt and tie, but never like this. Was this the real Nate? "I didn't mean to scare you."

"I didn't know you were up." His gaze dropped to her robe then quickly moved to her face. "Did you need something?"

"I heard movement. Can't sleep?"

He picked up the pencils he'd scattered on the ground.

"Nightmare again?"

He rested the pencils on the table, then sat.

"Still don't want to talk about it?"

He gathered the sketches he'd left on the table. She muttered something rude in French.

"I heard that."

"Good."

She grabbed a sketch before he could reach it. "Who are you?"

"What do you mean?"

"You're good at everything you do. You're successful in business, you speak French, you're a great valet, and now this. You're a true artist. Have you ever failed at anything?"

"Not yet," he said in a grave tone.

"Do you expect to?"

He turned away.

She jumped in front of him. "Nate, why won't you talk to me?"

"Have you ever been married?"

She paused, surprised by the change in subject. "No."

"Why not?"

"That's a personal question."

"Correct, and you have the right not to answer. That doesn't make you a bad person."

"And it doesn't make you a bad person to want to know more about someone."

"What's the point? We won't know each other in two weeks."

"But we know each other now. One thing I like about dogs is that they live in the moment."

He sat and returned to his sketch. "You better go back to bed, you have a busy day tomorrow."

Yvette rolled up her sleeves. "I'm going to figure you out if it kills me." She stood behind him, then gripped his shoulders.

"What are you doing?" he asked warily.

"I'm going to help you relax. I had a tense fox terrier once that I used to massage to ease his muscles and he loved it." She began working the muscles in his neck and shoulders. "You're very tense."

His tone deepened. "I know."

"Like a board."

"In more ways than one," he grumbled.

"What?"

"I think you should stop."

She shook her head, determined. "You're still tense."

"There's a reason for that."

"What reason?"

He jumped to his feet and faced her, his eyes like hot coals. "Careful, Yvette, you're going down a dangerous road."

She backed away. "What?"

"I'm not a little terrier that you can feed treats to, or a big Doberman that you can stroke, or a Labrador you need to pat on the head and say 'Good boy' to. I'm a man. A rational, logical man and I want you to know a few things about me." He took a menacing step toward her; she took a hasty step back. "I don't want your help." He took another step forward; she backed into the balcony railing. "I don't want your worry." He stopped a few inches in front of her, his dark gaze penetrating hers. "I don't want your thanks." He rested his hands on the railing behind her, trapping her in the circle of his arms. "And I don't want to want you." His mouth covered hers with the fierce, unrelenting force of an avalanche.

Yvette returned his kiss with just as much passion, wrapping her arms around his neck and arching her soft body into his hard form. He moaned, deepening the kiss and she let her arms fall to the muscles in his back, reveling in the feel of his warm flesh pressed against hers.

He drew away. "We should stop."

She pulled him close, wrapping one leg around his. "Why?"

He slid his arm around her waist. "You know why. I hadn't planned this."

She bit his earlobe and whispered, "Then you can write it into my schedule."

He shook his head. "We have to remember this is business. It's serious."

She touched the tip of his ear with her tongue. "I'm very serious about this."

"It's easy to fall in love in Paris."

She pulled away and stared up at him. "Have you done this before?"

"No." He kissed her again, then said in a hoarse voice, "I shouldn't be doing this."

Yvette tenderly touched his cheek, confused by his apparent torment. "Nate, we're two adults."

"This will change everything," he said, his voice a harsh whisper.

"You don't know that."

"Yes, I do." His eyes blazed down into hers. "I know what's at stake. If you sleep with me I guarantee you everything will change between us. Are you ready to take that risk?"

She nodded, not trusting herself to speak.

He cupped her face in his hands and searched her eyes. "Do you really believe in just living for today and not worrying about the future?"

"Yes," she said quickly, although she felt his question hid another one.

"Good." He stared up at the sky. "I defy you to meddle with me tonight. I'm going to enjoy this."

She smiled. "Who are you talking to?"

He returned his gaze to her face. "Fate. Destiny. We haven't been good friends for a while, but it doesn't matter now. Nothing matters, except this." He scooped her into his arms and took her to his bedroom. Once there, he placed her on the bed and unzipped his jeans. "There are a few things you should know about me."

"At last."

He removed his jeans, revealing a tight pair of dark blue briefs and well-defined thighs. He nodded to her robe. "Feel free to undress while I talk."

She leaned back and crossed her legs. "I

thought you might enjoy the pleasure." Yvette let her robe fall off her shoulder revealing the soft glow of her skin against the pink lace.

"I would, but I might rip something. I don't think you would want that."

Yvette pulled off her robe. "I could always buy another one." She undid the top of her boudoir, providing a small glimpse of her breasts. "What did you want to say?"

Nate stared at her as she sat half-naked on the bed.

"I forgot."

Yvette removed some of her clothes then smiled and rested on her side. "You were telling me about yourself."

Nate crawled onto the bed and pulled her toward him. She helped guide his hands as he took off her panties.

"Yes, that's right. I want you to know something. First, I don't like to share." He rolled on his back and wrapped both of his legs around hers. "I can be very possessive." His hand traced a slow seductive path down her back. "And I always take care of what belongs to me."

She wiggled against him. "Don't you have enough possessions?"

"Yes, but very few that I prize." He claimed her mouth again and made it clear how much he prized her, how much he wanted her and how much she now belonged to him. Yvette struggled not to feel overwhelmed by her own warring emotions. In his arms she felt both vulnerable and safe, a conqueror and a conquest. She'd never let herself get this close to a man. She'd always been confident with men who wanted her more than she wanted them, but her feelings for Nate shattered the secure wall that had kept that world at a distance. She'd only let animals this close to her heart and that fact terrified her, but the pleasure of his body soon pushed all fear away.

His roving lips took claim of her entire body from her chest to her thighs and the sacred space in between. She surrendered completely, aching for release. "Don't make me wait."

"I'm trying to get you ready," he said in a husky whisper between kisses.

"I am ready."

"Hmm, if you keep touching me like that this may end sooner than you think."

"That's a hint."

He didn't need any further instruction as Yvette invited him inside her. She was tight, but he didn't hesitate until she let out a light cry of surprise. He halted as though someone had just punched him in the gut.

"Yvette?" he said a little too quietly.

"What?"

"You're a virgin? Why didn't you tell me you've never done this before?"

"I didn't think it mattered."

He clenched his teeth. "Of course it matters. I would have done things differently."

"I like it just the way you're doing it." She continued to move her pelvis in motion with his.

He squeezed his eyes shut as though in pain and hung his head in defeat. "Fate strikes again."

She lightly kissed him. "Nate, I wanted this."

He opened his eyes. "Why me?" he asked in a raw voice.

She smiled, remembering his reply when she'd asked the same question weeks ago. "Why not?"

He buried his face in her neck. "Dear God."

"This isn't a mistake."

He shook his head. "I know, but—"

She stopped his words with a kiss. "We're only thinking about now, remember? There's nothing to worry about. Let's finish what we started."

"I'm going to go slow this time."

"Not too slow. I want to enjoy this."

"You're not only going to enjoy this, you're going to remember it."

His words were as good as a guarantee. When he moved inside her with firm but tender thrusts she thought he would slowly drive her out of her mind.

"Squeeze me," he said in a deep husky tone. "As though you never want me to leave." He groaned with pleasure as she tightened around him, the sound mingled with her own soft sigh of release. Neither wanted it to end, each desperate to satiate the primal hunger inside them while also pleasing the other. At last they collapsed in each other's arms, exhausted, languid and satisfied.

When Nate opened his eyes the first thing he noticed was that Yvette was gone. The second thing was the number on the digital clock. Two. But it was too bright to be two o'clock in the morning. He leaped out of bed and swore. It was two o'clock in the afternoon! He'd never slept that long. He paused for a moment as the realization hit him. *He'd actually slept?* There had been no nightmare, no waking up trembling, just pure perfect sleep. He could have wept with joy. He buried his face in his pillow to keep the tears from coming. Perhaps fate wasn't against him after all. Maybe Yvette was his one reprieve.

He sat up and swung his legs over the side of the bed. Yes, that had to be it. Yvette was the key and no matter how long they had together he was going to enjoy himself to the fullest. He quickly showered and dressed, hoping that by the time he'd finished Yvette would have returned. But when he left the bedroom she still wasn't there. His disappointment surprised him; he didn't expect to miss her this much. He cracked his knuckles and swore. He had to get ahold of himself.

How would she be when she saw him? Would she try to play it cool? Or make what happened last night mean more than it did? None of those scenarios pleased him. But he didn't want to play games.

He heard the jingle of keys in the door and quickly flopped on the couch, grabbing a magazine and pretending he was reading, instead of waiting for her.

"You're finally awake," Yvette said, coming into the room with several large bags.

"Yes."

She placed the bags down and sat next to him. She leaned over and gave him a sweet kiss on the cheek.

"That's an unusual skill."

"What?" He turned so she could kiss his other cheek.

She did, then tapped the magazine. "Reading upside down."

He glanced down. "Uh…yes." He tossed the magazine down, trying to remain casual. If she wouldn't mention last night, neither would he. "So how was your shopping?"

"Wonderful." She rummaged through one of her bags. "I bought you a present."

"Really?"

She pulled out a red-and-black lace teddy. "I bought two, just in case this one gets torn."

Nate grinned. He touched the fine lacy material, feeling the knot in his stomach relax. "This won't last five minutes."

She raised a brow. "I plan to find out tonight."

"You won't be disappointed."

She wasn't. They didn't see much of Paris on their last two days. Instead, they both enjoyed living in the moment—enjoying each other's company, making love and eating. Before leaving for home Yvette insisted that they visit Bernard to say goodbye.

"I don't think that's a good idea," Nate said packing his bag.

"We can't leave without telling him."

"He's a busy man. He won't mind." Nate spun around to grab a jacket from the closet, but the quick motion caught him off balance and he had to grab the dresser to keep from falling.

Yvette rushed up to him. "Are you okay?"

He shrugged her away. "I'm fine. Just a bit of vertigo."

Yvette watched him, concerned. It wasn't like him to be unsteady. "Perhaps you should stay here and I'll go see Bernard by myself."

"No," Nate said. "I don't want him to…" He sat on the bed and rubbed his hands over his face. "Why are you so stubborn?"

"I just want to say goodbye."

He let his hands fall and sighed, resigned. "Fine, we'll say goodbye on our way to the airport."

Yvette touched his forehead. "You look a little tired. I think you might be coming down with something."

He clasped her hand in his. "I'm fine, really. Don't worry about me. I just have a lot on my mind."

Yvette sat on his lap and wrapped an arm around his neck. "If you tell me what it is, I can help you."

"I don't want you to help me; it's my job to help you, remember?" He kissed her on the lips, then lifted her off his lap. "And I'm going to make sure you enjoy this experience."

"I am already. Nate, you don't have to do much more."

He flashed a rueful smile. "Except say good-bye to Bernard."

"Yes. Except that."

Bernard was sad to see them go and urged them to stay longer, but Nate refused. "She has events to attend in the States."

When Yvette left to use the restroom, Bernard said, "I'm happy to see that you've finally placed your cake in the oven. She's glowing."

Nate groaned. "You need another saying."

"You told her everything, no?"

"No."

Bernard's good humor vanished. "She cares about you. You will break her heart. You must tell her the truth."

"No."

"Why not? Are you afraid that she'll leave you or afraid that she'll stay? Have you spoken to your father? Or Kim?"

Nate shoved his hands in his pockets and shook his head. "I won't hurt her, I promise. I know what she wants."

Yvette returned, forcing Bernard to remain silent. He sighed, then hugged Nate goodbye. "I hope I will see you again soon." He turned to Yvette. "And you must try to look out for him and make sure he doesn't get into any trouble."

"I will do my best."

Nate walked to the door. "I'll tell Aunt Penny and Cathleen you said 'hello.'"

"Yes," Bernard said and waved goodbye as though he'd never see them again.

Chapter 11

When they returned back to his sister's apartment, they spent the first three days locked away.

"We can't stay in bed forever," Yvette said.

Nate lay on his stomach as she rubbed his back, which he had come to enjoy. Yvette found that he was a lot like James—protective, loyal and eager to please. Fortunately, he didn't snore. "I can," he mumbled.

"I can't ignore the phone calls. Your aunt called and so did Estelle."

"I said we have jet lag."

"Jet lag ends eventually."

"Hmm."

"Plus I have that function I'm supposed to take Queen to, remember?"

"It's a stupid dog birthday party."

"That your sister wants you to attend. Would you like to tell her that you didn't go?"

He sat up reluctantly. "No, but just wait. After attending a few parties here, you're going to wish you'd listened to me."

One thing Yvette did miss was getting a chance to call the shop and make sure things were going okay. She had so much she wanted to tell Lewis and Madlyn, but that would have to wait.

"It took me three days to decide on the trim," Mrs. Reynolds explained, examining a crocheted placemat on the buffet, not picking up on Yvette's expression.

It had taken Yvette only two seconds to decide the woman was a bore. Fortunately, the house made up for it. Last year it had been featured in *Architectural Digest* and it still looked photoworthy. Over the past week, Yvette had readjusted to Michigan time and had become adept at social chat. After the meeting at Ellen's she'd been given an official stamp of approval, and by disappearing to France for a week, returning and not talking to anyone, interest in her only grew so that when she finally emerged from her self-induced exile, her social calendar was filled with invites. There was the Needwoods' pet party where King and Queen dressed in costumes, the Hasbringer's charity auction where she only took Queen and now Ms. Reynolds's Spring Fling. Each event was grander than the last.

Yvette walked out to the garden where organza draped metal chairs, green silk cloth covered the tables and fire lanterns hung from the trees.

Nate handed her a glass. "Bored yet?"

"No." She sipped her drink. "Hmm. Delicious. You're a pro at this valet thing. Have you ever thought of a new line of work?"

He shook his head, his gaze roaming over her body. "I only like pleasing you."

"You're very good."

"I learn fast."

He also never left her side. Like a shadow he was always there, but never in her way. She was never without a chair, her food was perfect, her clothes perfect. The satin dress with matching shoes, pearl dinner bag and elegant opal earrings she wore had been laid out for her; all she had to do was show up and enjoy herself. But that didn't stop her from

wanting more. She knew it was a short-term
affair, but as the days passed sadness entered.
How would she say goodbye? She glanced at
Nate and watched as his dark eyes scanned the
crowd. She rested a light hand on his arm. "I
wish you would relax. You're my valet, not my
bodyguard."

Nate tried to smile, but failed. He couldn't
relax. It wasn't her fault. Yvette was easy to look
after. She never requested anything frivolous.
She was always enthusiastic and never complained. No matter how boring the conversation,
or tedious the evening, she always returned to the
apartment with a smile on her face.

He watched her even when he didn't want to.
He couldn't help himself. She was beautiful,
engaging and real. She cast a magical spell over
everyone she met. She was like a breath of fresh
air breezing through a room choked with expensive perfume and overinflated egos. He could
see how the other women watched her. Some
with admiration, others suspicion, and yet others
with jealousy. Nate thought about the dangerous
waters into which he'd thrown her.

He knew something was going on. Yvette had
been slighted but was too innocent to notice the
cool replies and smug glances. But Nate knew
and felt them intently. It started with the

Needwood party. Somehow they discovered that they didn't have enough plates for all the guests and to cover up the mistake, and to help save the reputation of the catering company, Yvette pretended to have already eaten and went home hungry that night. Although the dogs ate well. Nate ended up stopping at a diner to get some food. At the Hasbringer's there weren't enough chairs. Yvette ended up sitting on a stool at the children's table. Yvette was unaware of these mishaps but Nate knew the community was sending a message. One evening as he waited outside by the limos, a group of chauffeurs confirmed his suspicions.

"It's that new young one they can't stand," he overheard one say.

"Yeah, trying to get in with them," another added.

"They're teaching the poor girl a lesson and she doesn't even know it."

A third piped up. "She's donated a bunch of money to two organizations that aren't even real."

"She's just a rich sucker," the first chauffer said, then they all laughed.

Nate didn't find it funny at all. The game would end tonight. He waited to see what minor error would occur. He didn't have to wait long.

"Oh, no," Mrs. Reynolds exclaimed, as though a catastrophe was eminent.

"What is it?" Yvette asked.

"The bartender can't make it. All the guests will be here soon and it will just be awful."

"Perhaps you could call another company."

She tilted her head to the side. "Didn't you use to bartend, my dear?"

"Only for a while," Yvette said, a little stunned that she had that information.

She smiled. "A while is better than nothing. Would you mind?" She gestured to the bar.

She handed Nate her glass. "I suppose I could—"

Nate took the glass and Yvette's arm. "No, you couldn't." He turned. "We're leaving. Now."

Yvette stared at him. "But I don't mind."

"I do." He shuttled her into the house and found where the housekeeper had taken their coats.

Yvette looked at him, confused. "What's this all about?"

"Wait here."

"But—" He left before she could finish.

Yvette stood in the hall, stunned, then she heard a loud scream. She raced to the living room and saw Mrs. Reynolds, her face nearly the color of a pomegranate. "What is this?" she demanded, pointing to the floor. "My antique wood floor is destroyed. You stupid, stupid girl!"

"I'm sorry, Mrs. Reynolds," the maid replied. She was a young girl, with ebony skin and short-cropped hair. Yvette looked at the floor, but didn't see anything.

"There is an enormous scratch!"

The girl stood paralyzed. "Perhaps a rug—"

"A rug! Maybe I should just install carpeting and forget the whole thing."

"I didn't mean to."

"I don't care. Do you know what I will have to do to replace this? I can't believe you couldn't move a simple couch without damaging my floors. How many times do I have to tell you to use the utmost care?"

"But I—"

"Shut up!" She took off one of her shoes and threw it at the young woman. Fortunately, she was used to Mrs. Reynolds's outbursts and knew to duck. Unfortunately, Yvette didn't have that knowledge and the high heel grazed her face. She stumbled back in shock, a stinging sensation spreading on her cheek. She gingerly touched her fingers to her face and when she pulled them away she saw blood.

Mrs. Reynolds covered her mouth. "Oh, Yvette, I'm sorry, I was not aiming at you. I wanted to…"

Nate marched back into the room, hearing the commotion. "What's going on here?"

"There was a minor accident," Mrs. Reynolds said, dismissing him.

But Nate assessed the situation quickly seeing Mrs. Reynolds barefoot and the shoe near Yvette. "You'll hear from our lawyer." He adjusted Yvette's coat and dabbed the small trickle of blood with a napkin he grabbed off a nearby table. Mrs. Reynolds was aghast that he was using one of her possessions.

Mrs. Reynolds sniffed in disdain. "Don't be ridiculous."

"I've never found the charge of assault and battery ridiculous," Nate said softly.

She blinked uneasy. "I'm sorry. It wasn't intentional. I wasn't aiming at Yvette. It was that wretched creature." She pointed in the direction of Ayo, the maid, who stood frozen in place.

"What can I do?"

"You and your friends can stop playing games. The next time there are not enough plates or chairs, or you need to hurt someone, you'll hear from me. Do I make myself clear?"

"I'm truly sorry," Mrs. Reynolds said.

"I expect you to prove it." He turned to Ayo. "Where is your first-aid kit?"

"In the closet. I'll go get it."

"Perhaps you should sit down," Mrs. Reynolds said, trying to be nice. She motioned to the butler, who was standing off to the side, to assist them.

Nate shot her an ugly look. "Go back and deal with your bartender crisis. I'll take care of her." He led Yvette to a cushion.

"No," Mrs. Reynolds cried. "Don't sit on those they're—"

Nate spun around, his voice terse. "What?"

She stumbled back, touching her necklace with nervous fingers. "Nothing." She hurried away.

Yvette looked at the pristine couch and hesitated. "Perhaps we should go into the bathroom. I would hate to bleed on anything and ruin it."

Nate gently pushed her down. "I don't care if you bleed over everything in this damn room. You're the purest thing in here." He moved her hand and looked at her cheek. "For a superficial cut you shouldn't be bleeding this much."

"It will clot soon."

Nate looked around impatiently. "Where *is* that girl?"

"It's a large house."

"I don't care."

"Nate, your temper."

"I don't have a temper."

"I found it," Ayo called from the doorway.

Nate held out his hand, annoyed. "Please don't run. Take your time."

Ayo ran forward, unused to a valet speaking with such command.

"Thank you," Yvette said when Nate failed to say so.

"I need some water," he said. "And I want it cold."

Ayo placed her hands on her hips. "I don't take orders from—"

"You will take them from me."

"Nate—" Yvette warned.

Ayo folded her arms. "I don't listen to men who are on their knees."

Nate rose to his feet; Yvette grabbed his hand and stepped into his view. Unfortunately, he was taller and looked over her head. She grabbed his chin. "I'm still bleeding."

He blinked and she could see him gathering himself. It wasn't like him to lose control.

"That's right," Ayo said with a sneer. "Take your orders."

Yvette squeezed his hand. She could feel him trembling but he didn't turn.

"You've trained him well."

Yvette could feel her own temper thinning, but decided to use the tone she used with surly clients. She knew it was better to soothe than argue. "Please. I could really use some water."

It worked. All signs of anger disappeared and Ayo nodded. "Okay," she said, then left.

Yvette shook her head and sat back down. "With an attitude like that it's no wonder she gets shoes thrown at her."

Nate didn't smile. "I wouldn't have missed her." He opened the first-aid kit and cut a piece of gauze. "I shouldn't have done this. I shouldn't have brought you into this."

"It's okay."

He glanced up at her. "No, you don't know."

"Yes, I do. I know about the forgotten dish and not enough chairs and now the missing bartender."

He looked at her, stunned. "But you never let on."

"I was mocked all through middle and high school remember? I know all about being slighted. But I don't care. I've met some wonderful people. I've seen wonderful things. Those who don't want me around never will, but they can't stop me from enjoying myself. It's Leonard White all over again."

He placed the gauze on her cheek. She winced. "I'm sorry," he said. "Who's Leonard White?"

"A guy I briefly dated. He was attractive and athletic. We were quite a pair until I discovered he'd dated 'mush mouth,' that's what I was called, on a dare. When I found out we broke up. He ended up missing me more than I missed him. I told you before I don't invest in people."

"You don't expect them to treat you fairly?"

She shrugged. "Sure. You'll notice I'm not upset but you are. You're used to people treating you a certain way. Personally, I'm surprised. I'm surprised I'm even here. I'm even more surprised that people care that much about me, or are that interested in who I am to engage in silly games."

"Hmm."

She tapped him on the shoulder and playfully scolded him. "But you're going to blow our cover if you don't behave."

"What?"

"Remember. I'm the society lady. You're the valet. You can't start giving orders."

He let out an audible sigh. "I get protective when it comes to you."

"You'll spoil me."

His serious gaze captured hers. "Impossible."

Ayo returned. "Here's your water." She handed it to Yvette.

"What's your name?" Nate asked.

The maid resumed her aggressive stance. "Why do you want to know?"

"Because I'd like to apologize. I'm sorry about before. I shouldn't have been impatient with you."

Her arms fell to her sides in shock. Then, in a barely audible voice she said, "That's all right."

"No, it's not. I behaved badly." He turned to Yvette. "Come. Let me take you home."

"You can't be leaving!" a voice boomed.

They both turned and saw Ellen coming through the door. She tossed her coat at Ayo and held her hand out to Yvette. "I've been looking forward to speaking with you again. My goodness, what happened to your face? Never mind, I already know. Everyone's been witness to Lily's tantrums."

"We were getting ready to leave," Nate said.

"But you've just changed your mind." She took Yvette's arm and looked at Nate. "I'll take care of her from now on. Go and do what your type usually does, but don't roam too far."

Yvette sent Nate a helpless look as Ellen led her away. "I see you have a little bulldog." She patted Yvette's sleeve. "It's not a complaint, just an observation. I need you to do me a favor. The speaker for the Care for Animals charity had a family emergency to deal with and I would love you, if you agree, to replace her."

"Me?"

"All you have to do is introduce the guests and make a speech."

"But—"

Ellen flashed a brilliant smile. "I'm so glad you'll do this. Your experience working with animals and owning a successful dog-grooming salon makes you the perfect host. The event will be in a couple of days. And don't worry, there will be a teleprompter for you to read from."

Panic blocked out Yvette's memory of the rest of the party and it still lingered on her drive home and when she reached the apartment.

"What's wrong?" Nate asked her when she fell on the couch and ignored James who eagerly waited to be petted.

"Ellen wants me to speak, perhaps even read, at the Care for Animals charity at the end of the week. She wouldn't let me refuse. I can't do that."

He sat down beside her. "Of course you can."

"I can't. You heard me read."

"You read well."

"But not perfectly. I can't read in front of a whole bunch of people. I'll just have to get sick."

"You'll be talking about a subject you care about. I thought you said you wanted to be the voice for animals."

"Why me? It's strange. She hardly knows me. Maybe she wants to see me fail."

"You're not going to fail and she selected you because you are a good draw."

Yvette frowned. "A good draw?"

"You're rich and great to look at. The cameras will love you."

Her panic grew. "There are going to be cameras?"

Nate drew her close. "You'll be fine. You're a very attractive, extremely wealthy—at least that's what they think—woman with ties to the event's coordinator, that's enough." He paused "By the way, rumor has it that you are a multimillionaire."

"Who started that?"

He shrugged.

"It doesn't matter what they think." Yvette rested her head against him. "It's not enough."

"Yvette, it's no big deal."

"Yes, it is," she said with tears building in her eyes.

"Why?"

"Because Ellen said that it's in a few days."

"So?"

So my month with you ends in a few days and this stupid event will be held on our last night together. A tear fell. She angrily brushed it aside. "Nothing. I'm just afraid."

Nate tenderly brushed her cheek with his knuckles. "You'll be fine. I've always taken care of you, haven't I? I'll be with you at the charity. By the time I'm finished coaching you, you'll be a pro. Let me go over your speech and make any changes, if needed, just to make sure it'll be easy for you to read. I'll take care of everything. Trust me."

That wasn't the problem. Yvette trusted him, but loving him was worse. Lately, she'd found herself watching him, wanting to be with him. Like James, who after first meeting Nate followed him everywhere. Luckily, some of her apprehension lessened the next day when Nate told her he had gotten the speech from Ellen. He spent the rest of the day replacing difficult words with simpler ones, creating a smoother rhythm. As soon as he was finished he handed it to Yvette and sat on the couch with King, Queen and James.

Yvette excused herself, "Let me go over it first, before doing it in front of an audience." At first Yvette felt self-conscious and awkward. The words felt like stones in her mouth and her anxiety rose. She didn't see Nate and the three dogs, instead she saw a classroom full of high-school kids laughing at her. The sound of their jeers ripped holes in her heart, then, suddenly she saw a well-dressed crowd in front of her, filled with people who had advanced degrees and perfect speech waiting to see her fail.

But she wouldn't fail. She had come too far. Determined to silence them forever, Yvette took a deep breath and began. When she was finished, Nate applauded her performance, but inside she still didn't feel prepared. She knew that she needed help if she was to survive the event, so she called Rania to schedule an appointment.

Rania agreed, "At last. I've been waiting to hear from you."

Chapter 12

"You're not paying attention," Rania said. "You've hardly listened to a word I've said."

"I'm sorry."

"What's the matter?"

Yvette shook her head. "It's nothing. I'm just nervous."

"No, you're depressed. What's wrong?"

"I don't think I can do it."

"Yes, you can."

"You don't understand. When I was a child—"

"But you're no longer a child," Rania said with an impatient move of her shoulders. "You are now a woman. I know about your past, Yvette, but it doesn't have to stop you. You said you wanted respect and people to listen to what you said. Now you have that chance; don't throw it away. Do you remember the oath?"

"Yes."

"Then say it."

"As a member of The Black Stockings Society, I swear I will not reveal club secrets. I will accept nothing but the best and I will no longer settle for less."

"But what does that have to do with now?"

"Fear makes people settle. You're settling to be the old Yvette who just observed and envied the life she wanted to live. This is your chance to seize it. You can do this. Public speaking is all about control. Nothing more. You've handled packs of dogs, disgruntled owners, conniving rich widows and self-centered millionaire bachelors. The people who will be attending this function love animals as much as you do. They will want to listen to you. Now let's get to work."

For the next two hours Rania gave Yvette tips on how to stand at the podium, the importance of movement, how to engage an audience, clarity of voice and how to project it. At one point she had Yvette blowing into a tiny glass bottle, forcing her to use her abdominal muscles. After Yvette repeated the speech ten or more times, Rania pronounced her ready.

"You and I both know you'll be representing more than the charity. You'll be representing The Black Stockings Society. Make us proud. You never know who will be watching." She smiled, a little sad. "You probably don't need the club anymore."

"You mean I'll no longer be a member?"

"You'll always be a member, just not in the same way. Your future is all up to you now. Wait here," Rania instructed as Yvette reached for her coat. While she waited Yvette felt the overwhelming sense of sorrow return. She knew that Friday night would be the end of everything: her time with Rania, The Black Stockings Society and knowing Nate. She tried hard to fight back the tears. She wasn't ready for this.

Rania reappeared a few minutes later, holding a large, closed garment bag. "Wear these to the event. Don't open it until that night."

Yvette nodded as though she were a robot. "Thank you."

Rania sat on the couch and patted the space beside her. Yvette reluctantly sat. "Tell me what's really bothering you."

"I don't know."

"Lying doesn't help anything. You need to be honest. If not to me, at least to yourself."

In between tears and awkward laughter, Yvette revealed the truth: her true desires and her hopes of allowing the real her, not the one who was skillful at playing at being rich, to shine through.

Rania nodded when she was finished. "That's the Yvette who was invited to join The Black Stockings Society."

"And there's no way to know who nominated me?"

Rania shook her head. "Your success is thanks enough."

Yvette cried all the way home. When she got to the parking garage, she sat in her car and cried some more. When she couldn't cry anymore, she sat for several more minutes. She was ready. Yes, she hurt, but she was happy. The plan had worked, and she would always remember this time of her life. She took out the eyedrops she kept in her bag, hoping to reduce the redness in her eyes.

But her eyes didn't matter when she saw Nate holding tissues to his nose. "What happened?"

"I tripped over James and crashed into the door."

"Put your head back."

"No, I'm all right. The bleeding stopped." He threw the tissue away.

She studied him for a moment, then felt his forehead. "You feel a little warm."

He laughed. "It's embarrassment," he said, then looked at her, puzzled. "Are you all right?"

"Why?"

"Your eyes are red."

She hugged him and whispered, "Yes, I'm fine. I just got something in my eye." She kissed him and he kissed her back, neither wanting to admit that they'd soon say goodbye.

She was about to change for bed when the phone rang. "Hello?"

"Hi, it's Cathleen. I was wondering if you could do me a favor."

"What?"

"Can you take Lewis as your date to the Care for Animals charity? I would take him myself, but my mother would kill me. This is the only way I can get him invited. Please, for me."

Yvette looked at Nate, who was watching her from his side of the bed. "I don't know."

"Do you have another date?"

She hesitated. "No."

"Please, Yvette. I'll make it up to you. I just need this one favor."

Yvette sighed. "All right."

"Thank you. I'll tell Lewis. He'll meet you at your place then you can come together."

"Right." Yvette hung up, shaking her head.

"What?" Nate asked.

"I have a date for the charity."

Nate scowled. "With whom?"

"Lewis. I'm doing this as a favor to Cathleen."

"I'll still drive you."

"I don't need both you and Lewis."

"I'll drive you."

She knew when it was best not to argue.

On the night of the event, Yvette was a bundle of nerves. But the way she looked did not reveal any of her panic. When she opened the garment bag Rania had given her, she was speechless. Inside was a pretty, satin aqua suit, with braided satin trim that added unexpected detail to the jacket lapel, ending in a shimmering cascade. The matching straight skirt had a back walking slit that showed off her third pair of stockings. They were shimmering off-black with rhinestones that formed a seam down the back. Nate didn't say anything when he saw her, but Lewis couldn't help himself.

"Men of Michigan, look out. Ms. Coulier is on the prowl tonight. You look sensational. Don't you think so, Nate?"

"Yes." He held the door open for them to enter the car.

"I shouldn't even be doing this," Yvette said, adjusting her hemline. Lewis couldn't help noticing how sensuous her legs looked.

"What's wrong with helping out a friend? I really like her." He adjusted his seat and looked at her.

"Really?"

"I'm serious, Yvette."

"Good, because so is Cathleen."

"Thanks for doing this."

"I'm not doing it for you." Yvette looked away.

"For your information, Cathleen means a lot to me."

"It's only been a month."

"A lot can happen in a month." He lowered his voice. "I've seen the way you look at Nate." Yvette didn't turn. She just kept looking out the window.

"Everyone looks at Nate like that. They can't help it."

Yvette knew it wouldn't be an ordinary night the moment she entered the grand hall. The throng of photographers and reporters made any movement nearly impossible. Once they discovered who she was, everyone wanted her picture. Nate, who was very adept at avoiding cameras, guided her through the crowd, leaving Lewis to fend for himself.

Cathleen stood waiting for them. "You look great. Wow, those stockings are unbelievable."

"Thank you. You look wonderful, too."

She blushed. "Thanks. Where's Lewis?"

A hand appeared above the crowd. "I'm coming."

Cathleen touched Yvette's arm. "I'm so glad you're doing this for me."

"You're welcome." Love had changed Cathleen. She looked lovely in a dress that fit, and Yvette noticed how her face shone and the way she carried herself.

Lewis finally emerged. "It's like trying to get through a forest."

"I'm glad you could come," Cathleen said.

He kissed her on the cheek. "I wouldn't have missed it."

They began to hold hands, but Ellen pounced on the small group.

"There you are, Yvette! You're just as stunning as I'd hoped you'd be. We're going to make a killing tonight." She took Yvette's arm and glanced at Lewis. "Are you her date for the evening?"

"Yes."

She looped her arm through his. "Good. You

two make a very attractive couple. Come with me. I'll show you where you'll be sitting." She led them to a reserved table. It was only after Lewis and Yvette had been seated that Ellen noticed Nate standing nearby. She smiled at him. "I haven't forgotten about you. I'll be back." She sauntered off.

"You can't just stand there," Yvette said.

"I'm not in anyone's way."

"You're making me nervous."

Lewis fought to see through the crowd. "Did you see where Cathleen went?"

Nate nodded. "Yes, her mother dragged her to the far table over there."

Lewis frowned. "So much for our brilliant plan."

"There will be enough time for the two of you to sneak off later."

Ellen returned and took Nate's arm. She looked at Yvette. "Do you mind?"

"Not at all."

Yvette tried not to laugh as she led Nate away.

"Can you believe we're in a place like this?" Lewis said.

"It is amazing." Yvette looked at the trays full of exotic cheeses and hors d'oeuvres and the different drink concoctions available at the bar.

"This is the way to live. I don't think I could ever go back."

"It's a shame that Cathleen couldn't be sitting here instead of me."

Lewis shrugged. "It's all right. You heard Nate. I'll get to see her later."

"She looks lovely tonight," Yvette said, a bit surprised that he hadn't said anything. "She's really come out of her shell. What do you like most about her?"

"Everything."

Before Yvette could challenge him to be more specific the lights dimmed and Ellen approached the podium. She welcomed everyone and expressed how delighted she was with the turnout. Yvette didn't hear a word. Her heart was beating too fast. She just wanted it to be over.

Lewis nudged her. "Yvette, she just called you."

Yvette jumped to her feet and approached the podium like a wooden doll. She adjusted the microphone and looked out but saw only darkness. Relieved that she didn't have to look into anyone's face, she glanced at the teleprompter, ready to begin. Then she saw the words and froze.

They were different. It wasn't the speech that she had practiced. Panic gripped her and at that moment there was no Nate to offer her comfort or even Rania to tell her what to do. She gripped the side of the podium, wondering whether she

should run off the stage or faint. Then out of the
corner of her eye she saw a familiar figure:
Margaret. But this wasn't the Margaret she remembered. This Margaret wore a striking green
hat and glittery dress. Margaret nodded her en-
couragement and Yvette gathered courage as she
remembered Rania's words: "You will be representing The Black Stockings Society."

Yvette opened her mouth and began. The
speech was flawless. She even added some lines
that had been in the original speech Nate had
written. Resounding applause followed and she
left the stage feeling renewed. She had buried the
old frightened Yvette, the one with the speech
impediment and no friends, forever.

Many people wanted to meet her and overwhelmed her with their need for attention. She
tried to find Margaret but failed. Fortunately
she didn't let her disappointment dampen the
evening. Lewis and Cathleen managed to escape
for some alone time together and Yvette became
the most popular woman in the room. The
evening improved from there.

At least for Yvette. Nate wasn't having as
good a time. This was his last night with her and
he hadn't been able to manage a minute alone
with her. After her speech he'd wanted to jump
on the stage and kiss her. But instead he'd been

relegated to the back of the room. For once in this whole damn plan he wished he wasn't her valet.

He wanted to claim her. He wanted to be sitting at the table where Lewis had been. He wanted to have Ellen say what a good-looking couple they were. But he'd had to keep his mouth shut and watch another man take his place.

That's what bothered him most. Once he was gone he knew another man would replace him. Yvette didn't have to stay alone for very long if she didn't want to. The thought gnawed at him.

He hadn't slept well last night or the other six nights. The reason wasn't nightmares. It was Yvette. She filled his thoughts. And he wasn't thinking of her schedule. He wasn't thinking about her clothes or her meals. He was thinking of her smile, her legs, her sleeping in the bed beside him and how it was all going to end one day.

That day had arrived and he wasn't handling it as indifferently as he would have liked. He wanted to be casual about it, nonchalant. But he couldn't. He gripped his hand, forming a fist. This was his last night with Yvette and he was going to seize it. But first he would have to find her. He pushed his way through the crowd.

"I didn't expect to see you here," a female voice said in amazement.

Nate turned and saw Ayo, the maid from Mrs.

Reynolds's house. She noticed his surprise. "I took your advice and quit. This job doesn't pay the same as working for that witch, but at least I don't get the same treatment."

"Good." He turned to leave.

She touched his arm. "You know, I have a day off tomorrow."

He glanced away. "I'm busy."

"She's out of your league."

He turned to look at her. "What?"

"The lady you work for. I've seen the way you watch her, and trust me, I've seen other guys look at her the same way. If she has the choice, she'll choose the guy who can pick up the tab, not her laundry. Just a thought." She turned over his palm and scribbled down her number. "Just in case you come to your senses."

"Right," Nate said, then weaved his way outside, but Yvette wasn't there. He looked around but couldn't find her.

"I had hoped to find you," Ellen said. "You look lost."

"I'm looking for Yvette."

"Don't worry; she's being well taken care of. But as you can see, I've been neglected." Neglecting Ellen was impossible. Nobody could miss the ravishing woman whose red dress put nearly every other woman to shame.

Nate thought it best not to reply.

"I pay very well."

"I'm happy where I am."

She moved closer. "You could always be happier."

"Thank you. I'll keep that in mind."

She touched his face, then his leg. "Yes, do."

"There you are," Cathleen said. "Yvette needs you."

"Excuse me." Nate rushed over to her, relieved. "Where is she?"

Cathleen motioned to a small enclosure. "I don't know. I just thought you needed a little help." She nodded toward Ellen. "I see you're still getting into trouble."

He shoved his hands in his pocket, thankful for the rescue. "It's not my fault."

"Yes, women can't help but find you irresistible. But you care for only one."

"Don't speak in code."

"I don't think I need to speak at all."

"Good." He began to walk away.

"Are you going to look for her?"

"No." He was tired of looking for her. Of seeing her and having her out of reach. He couldn't make the evening become something that it wasn't meant to be, just like he couldn't change fate. "I'm going for a walk."

* * *

On the drive home, both Yvette and Nate let Lewis do all the talking. They said their goodbyes to him in the parking lot, then Lewis drove away and Nate and Yvette returned to the apartment. James eagerly greeted their return while King and Queen briefly brushed against them, then returned to their comfortable positions on the rug.

Nate watched Yvette sit on the couch ignoring James's request to be petted. "It was a perfect evening and you were a tremendous success. Why are you so quiet?"

She stared out the window. "I guess the finality of all this is hitting me. Tomorrow we go our separate ways."

Nate sat on the other end of the couch. "We knew this was only for a time," he said in a quiet voice.

Yvette folded her arms. He was right. Unfortunately his words didn't stop her heart from breaking. "Yes."

"My life is back East."

She gave a brief nod. "I know."

"You've made great connections and have plenty of money left. You can still shop and travel—"

"It's not enough," she said in a flat tone.

"What do you mean it's not enough? I've given you everything you've ever wanted. We had an agreement and I—"

Yvette jumped to her feet and shouted at him. "I know all that! I know about our damn agreement. I know I have the clothes and the connections and the money I've always wanted, but it doesn't matter right now because I love you and I can't stop you from leaving me." She spun away, not wanting him to see her flow of tears.

"Yes, you can."

She paused, but did not turn. "What?"

Yvette heard him get up from the couch and briefly closed her eyes as his footsteps grew near. Then she felt his hands on her shoulders. She kept her gaze to the floor when he turned her to face him. "Yvette," he said softly like a caress.

"I don't want to talk about it. I don't want to hear you say you can stay another week or another month because it won't be enough."

"I know."

She gazed up at him startled. "You do?"

"Yes." His words were barely a whisper. "Will you marry me?"

She backed away from him, certain she'd misunderstood. "Is this some sort of joke?"

"No. Please don't look at me like that. I wouldn't tease you this way."

"But I don't understand."

He took a deep, steadying breath, but when he spoke the strength of his emotions made his voice shake. "You've captured my heart and I've never been happier in my life. I wasn't sure what my future would be until I met you. Money didn't change you. I was afraid that it would, but it didn't. I've learned that not everyone can be corrupted by wealth, and that living in the moment is a gift. I want to spend the rest of my life with you. All that's mine will be yours. You allowed me to take care of you for one month. Now I want to take care of you for the rest of my life. What do you say?"

Yvette clasped her hands together, but it didn't stop her from trembling. It wasn't his words that held her entranced; it was his face. She thought she had seen all the expressions that could cross his face, but she had never seen this one. She recognized the emotion that caused it—fear. He had never faced failure before and she had power over him. The power to say "no." She knew he didn't give his power away lightly. "You love me?"

He nodded.

She fell on the couch and burst into tears.

He stared at her helpless. "Yvette?"

"It's too much to believe. I can't believe this is happening to me."

"But it's real. Please don't make me wait for an answer."

She leaped to her feet and threw her arms around him. "The answer is yes." She kissed him and he kissed her back and soon King and Queen had to make room for them on the rug. Yvette stopped before they went too far.

"We could break something," she said, zipping up her dress.

He unzipped it again. "My sister will forgive me."

She began to stand. "We can finish in the bedroom."

He pulled her down. "I want to finish here."

"No."

"Is this how you're going to treat me *after* we're married?"

"After we're married we'll have our own place and I won't care where we make love, but I don't want to do it here."

She tried to stand again, but he locked his arm around her waist. "There's just one thing."

"What?"

"I don't want to tell anyone until after we're married. We'll have to do a quick, quiet ceremony."

"Why? Are you ashamed to introduce me to your family?"

He shook his head. "No, it's not that. It would just be better for me this way. We can have a big ceremony later, but for now I just want us and a justice of the peace. We can have our honeymoon in Paris and travel to all the countries you've ever wanted to see."

She hesitated.

"Trust me. Let me take care of everything. You trusted me before. We can get a license, then fly to Vegas and get married by next week. Please? I won't ask you for anything more after this."

"Okay," she said with some reluctance. "If it means that much to you. But can I at least tell my two friends Lewis and Madlyn?"

He thought a moment. "Sure. What could go wrong?"

Chapter 13

Cathleen stared at Lewis, stunned, as they sat in her favorite restaurant. "Get married?"

"Sure, why not?"

"But we've only known each other a few weeks."

"But I feel like I've known you my whole life. Don't you feel it, too?"

"Yes, but—"

"I know it seems a little crazy, but we wouldn't be the only ones. Yvette and Nate are getting married."

"What!"

"Yes, she just told me yesterday." He put a finger to his lips. "But it's supposed to be a secret so don't tell anyone."

"I can't believe this."

"So do you want to get married?"

She wrung her hands. "I...don't know."

"I thought you loved me."

"I do love you, but—"

"And with me as your husband you won't be pushed around by your mother anymore. Don't you want to live in your own house and come and go as you want and do what you want?"

"Yes."

"Then marry me." He held both of her hands in his.

Cathleen looked down at his hands, her mind racing. He treated her so well and no other man had ever paid attention to her like he had. Well, one had, but not like this. "All right."

Lewis would have jumped for joy if he could have, but instead he squeezed her hands tighter. "You won't regret it. I think we should elope, that way no one can stand in our way."

"Elope?"

"Yes. This weekend. Pack your things and meet me here." He bent over and kissed her. "I love you so much and now we can be together forever."

Lewis continued talking about his plans for them, but Cathleen wasn't listening. Although she looked forward to a life filled with her own happiness all she could think about was Nate's decision and why he'd kept it a secret from her. At home she called him, requesting they meet.

She selected a jazz club where no one could see them. When Nate saw her he smiled and took a seat. "This isn't like you. Why did you want to see me so urgently?"

"I'm getting married."

His expression changed. "To whom? Lewis? Isn't that rather sudden?"

She raised her brows. "No more sudden than your marriage to Yvette."

He swore.

"Lewis told me. My question is why didn't you?"

"You know why. You'll tell Aunt Penny, she'll tell Dad, Dad will tell Kim and before you know it you will all try to talk me out of it."

"We care about you. We want to see you happy."

"I am happy."

"Have you told Yvette—"

"No, but I'm going to. I promise."

"This isn't fair to her."

"Look, she'll understand when I explain it to her, but I want to explain it in my own way."

"After you're married?"

"Yes."

Cathleen shook her head. "That's not right."

"She's not like the rest of you. She'll understand." He stood.

"So you've made your decision."

"Yes, and it's final."

Nate didn't return home immediately. Instead he walked the night streets trying to get his thoughts in order. He knew that Cathleen didn't understand, nobody did and he didn't want to try to make them. This was what he wanted and he wouldn't let anyone or anything stand in his way. He only had a few more days and then everything would be final. He and Yvette would be married, then off to Paris away from his family and anyone who would try to interfere.

When he finally reached home, he saw Yvette wiping James's face with a towel. "Did he get into our dinner or something?"

"No, I'm just wiping his eyes. You have to do this often with this breed because they are prone to eye troubles. Where were you?"

He patted both King and Queen, who came up to greet him then went into the kitchen. "Cathleen told me she's getting married."

"What?" Yvette followed him into the kitchen with James close behind. "To Lewis?"

Nate poured himself a drink. "Yes, she said he got the idea from us."

"Us?" Yvette thought for a moment then covered her eyes and groaned. "Oh, no."

"That's why I didn't want you to tell anyone."

"But Lewis never seemed like the marrying type."

Nate swallowed his drink then set the glass in the sink. "The fact is he told her about us. She can keep it a secret for a while, but not for too long. We'll leave for Vegas Friday instead of Saturday."

Yvette shrugged. "Okay. Are you worried about her?"

He left the kitchen and sat on the arm of the couch. "No, she seems to know what she's doing."

"I wonder if Lewis does."

"If they want to get married, we can't stop them. We're certainly not the ones to tell them not to. They're two adults."

Yvette dropped on the couch. "Yes."

"You don't sound convinced."

"It's just that Lewis has never thought or even talked about marriage before."

Nate smiled. "Neither did I. If you had met me

a few months ago you wouldn't believe me right now." He slid down beside her. "In a few days you're going to be Mrs. Nate Blackwell and then we'll be on our way to Paris."

A couple days later as they sat on the balcony, Yvette could feel nothing but happiness. Yesterday she and Nate had gone to Belle Isle. They had spent the day playing with the dogs and he had sketched them and her; she had made him a cherry pie. The day before that they'd visited the lakeshore and enjoyed the miles of beach and now they sat together quiet in each other's company knowing there would be more days, no, years, like this.

"Diana will be returning soon," Nate said. "We can't stay here."

"You can slum it for a while at my place."

"Maybe, or I'll set us up in a hotel while we look for a place."

"You'll move to Michigan?"

"Sure. You want to stay, right?"

"Yes, but isn't your business and everything back East?"

"It will survive without me. Don't worry, the money won't run out."

She hated when he talked about money that way. "That's not what I meant. I mean you have an entire life back there. You can't just pick up and move. Won't you miss it?"

"Not really. I can always visit. My life is here now, with you. You can still run Le Chic Hounds and get involved with other charities."

"It just seems like you're giving up a lot."

"No. I came here to make a decision about whether I'd go back or not and I've made it. My life is here."

"Okay," she said, unsure.

"You just have to tell me where you want to live. I'd like something by the water."

"Me, too." He looked so excited she felt guilty for the niggling worry gnawing at her. She didn't like how quickly he was cutting himself off from his past. Why didn't he want anyone to know about them? Why did he want to get married so quickly? What was he running away from?

Two days later, Yvette continued to ponder these questions. She sat in Le Chic Hounds helping Madlyn with inventory when Estelle came in with Lucy.

"Hello, Estelle!" Madlyn said. She whispered to Yvette, "She comes in almost every week and spends."

"Your favorite type of customer."

"You better believe it."

Estelle walked up to them. "Ooh, that looks interesting."

"It's a new line of bowls." Madlyn went on to

describe their special features while Yvette stacked them.

"It sounds just perfect for my Lucy. I would like one, please."

Madlyn dashed over to the cash register. "I'll ring you right up."

Estelle stayed with Yvette. "You know you're always welcome to attend our weekly meetings."

"Thank you."

"I know you don't really need us. You have a full life. With your business and fabulous valet," she said with a teasing grin. "I saw that you met Marshall Post. Did you get a new puppy?"

"What?"

"At the Care for Animals charity. I saw you with Marshall."

"You must be mistaken. I didn't get to meet him."

"Yes, you did. You were sitting right next to him almost all evening."

Fear twisted her heart. "Lewis?"

"I don't know what name he used with you, but that was definitely him. I never forget a face. Especially one as handsome as his."

Yvette couldn't move. Lewis was the con artist? The puppy mill culprit? *He* was scamming rich women into buying non-breed dogs? It suddenly all made sense. The expensive clothes and watches he wore that he could never have afforded on a struggling photographer's salary. She finally understood why he'd been so interested in her relationship with Nate and his sudden attention to Cathleen. She had to do something. She couldn't let the marriage happen.

"Wow, Yvette, you've really done well for yourself," Lewis said, glancing around the apartment.

She took his jacket. "This isn't my place."

He walked into the living room, ignoring James's low growl. "But now you can afford one like it." He sat on the couch. James followed and sat in front of him. Lewis turned away. "Where's Nate?"

"He's picking King and Queen up from Le Chic Hounds. Would you like anything to drink?"

"Do you have champagne? I feel like celebrating."

"I'll get you some apple juice."

He shrugged. "I'll get myself a bottle later." He threw up his hands in triumph. "Look at us. We can afford a lot of things now. Nate seems like a good guy and Cathleen's sweet. What the hell is wrong with your dog?"

"What is he doing?"

"He's staring at me."

"James, come here."

The dog didn't move. His gaze remained fixed on Lewis.

Lewis sniffed. "He's not very bright if he doesn't know his own name."

Yvette frowned and handed Lewis his glass. "James is very smart. I don't know why he's acting this way." She tugged on his collar. "Come on James, stop that. You've met Lewis before. He's nothing like Arthur." James made a sound of protest, but let Yvette lead him to her side. She sat on the couch and stroked his head. "Good boy. I want you to behave. Perhaps he thinks you're Nate's rival or something."

Lewis laughed and leaned toward the dog. "You have nothing to worry about."

James curled his lip, revealing his teeth.

Lewis jumped back. "Oh, well."

Yvette tapped James's nose. "Be good."

Lewis took a gulp of his drink, set the glass down, then stretched his arms out across the length of the couch. "So what did you want to see me about?"

"Nate told me you and Cathleen are getting married."

"Yes, isn't that great?"

"Yes, and very lucky. You're marrying a rich woman."

He lifted a brow in challenge. "And you're marrying a rich man."

"Because I love him."

Lewis rolled his eyes. "You wouldn't have given him the time of day if he didn't have money."

"That's not true."

"Look, if you asked me here to change my mind about Cathleen you're wasting your time. You can't talk her out of it, either, because she loves me. A lot. Tonight we're meeting at her favorite restaurant and running off together."

"No, you're not."

"What do you mean?"

"I know how you make your 'extra' money."

He finished his drink, then stared at the glass. "I don't know what you're talking about."

"I'm talking about how you have been using our store to gain access to rich dog lovers to scam them into buying phony designer dogs. I saw the dog you sold Estelle Walters."

He set his glass down. "So what? She looks happy, doesn't she?"

"It's illegal."

"After I've married Cathleen I'll stop. I won't have to run it anymore."

"You're not going to marry Cathleen."

He flashed a slow, cruel smile. "Yes, I am and no one is going to stop me."

Yvette boldly glared back. "I will."

He shook his head as though she were a foolish child. "Don't stand in my way, Yvette. I've dreamed about a chance like this."

"She deserves better."

"Nobody even looked at her before me. I make her happy. There's nothing wrong with getting paid for the privilege."

"You scheming, conniving pig. You don't even care about—"

"Who are you to tell me about caring? Who do you care about? And don't give me that garbage about loving Nate. You saw him and saw how rich he was and then started flashing your legs in high-priced stockings and dressing up like a fine lady. Don't tell me you went after him because he had a great mind."

"It wasn't like that."

"You've never looked at a man before. All you've ever cared about were animals. I know; I've been trying to get you to love me for years. But you've never seen me, never even considered how *I* felt or anyone. Men look at you and you take it for granted. I'm not going to be taken for granted anymore. It's a dog-eat-dog world out there and I'm fighting to get my fair share so you'd better stand out of my way." He headed for the door.

"If you go through with this, I'll tell everyone the truth."

He turned and shoved her against the wall, his hand around her throat. "Don't play games with me, Yvette," he warned in a low voice. "I don't want to hurt you, but I will."

Yvette started to see stars and seized his wrist, but he suddenly released his hold and let out a scream. She glanced down and saw James biting his leg. Lewis tried to shake him off, then grabbed a vase and hit him. James crumpled.

Yvette dropped to her knees, tears streaming down her face. "If you've killed him I swear I'll get you."

Lewis looked down at them in disgust. "Yes, I know how much you like animals. What do they call female dogs again?"

Yvette gently lifted James in her arm. "He's still breathing. I have to take him to the vet."

Lewis blocked her way. "First you have to promise me you won't say anything."

"No."

He removed a strand of hair from her face with his finger. "It would be a shame if you suddenly disappeared. I could put you in a place where Nate's money won't be able to find you."

"I'm not afraid of you. Now get out of my way."

"You have such a pretty face. I wonder if Nate

would want you anymore if something bad were to happen to it." He slapped her.

She stumbled back in shock.

"Still not afraid of me?"

Yvette placed James down and grabbed a broom. "I want you to leave."

"I could ruin everything for you. How would Nate feel if he came home and found us together?"

"I said get out."

"You can't force me." He glanced at James. "Your little protector is out of commission and there's no one else here to rescue you. I think you'd better start listening to me." He wrestled the broom from her and threw it on the ground. He grabbed her arms and pulled her close, his breath hot on her face. "Come on. You want to care about somebody? What about caring about me? Who's been your friend all these years? Who listened to your pathetic stories about your father and how no one liked you in school? Wasn't I always there? Huh?"

She struggled against him.

"I will kill you in two seconds if you do not let her go," Nate said in a quiet, deadly voice.

Lewis shoved Yvette away. "We were just playing a little game," he said, startled by Nate's sudden appearance.

Nate's gaze pierced the distance with a fury that stilled the air. "And we're going to play another game. You're going to get out of our lives—and Cathleen's—and we will never hear from you again."

Lewis scowled, but didn't speak. He grabbed his coat then stormed out. Once he was gone Yvette lifted James. His eyes had opened but didn't look focused. "He's hurt. We've got to get him to a vet."

Nate saw the side of her face. "Did he hit you?"

She nodded then glanced down at James. "He also hit—"

Nate didn't give her a chance to finish. Within seconds he was out the door. He returned minutes later rubbing his knuckles. She noticed red spots on his shirt.

"Is that blood?"

"Don't worry, it's not mine."

"What did you do to him?"

"I doubt he'll remember."

"What does that mean?"

"It means I sent him home."

Yvette gasped and widened her eyes.

"No, I don't mean heaven," he said quickly. "I made sure he got in his car after making my point clear. He may stop at a hospital, but that's his decision." He took James from her. "Come on, let's go. You can tell me what happened."

Cathleen looked at her watch for the fourth time. Lewis should have been there by now.

"Hi, Cathleen," Nate said taking a seat.

"What are you doing here?"

"Keeping you company."

"You don't need to. My bags are in the car and Lewis will be here in a minute."

He shook his head. "No, he won't."

"Yes, he will. He asked me to marry him. He wouldn't have changed his mind."

"It's my fault."

"What do you mean?"

"I wanted to make sure he really loved you so I told him that if he married you, you'd be disinherited."

She set her mouth firm. "He does love me."

"Then why isn't he here?"

"He's coming."

"Cathleen," he said gently. "He's not the only man out there."

"You're marrying Yvette and I didn't say anything. Why did you do this to me? You had no right! Do you think Yvette would marry you if you didn't have money?" she asked, her eyes filling with tears.

"It's different for me. I'm older and—"

"And selfish. You can have happiness and do whatever you want but I can't." She stood and raced out the door.

Nate returned to the apartment ready to fall into bed. He didn't feel tired, he felt weary. He wished he could have done more damage to Lewis but knew he'd never see him again. At least the vet had said James would recover completely. And Yvette was better and he knew Cathleen would take time to forgive him. He wasn't selfish. Maybe in the past but not now and he'd prove it.

When he opened the door, Yvette met him.

"A woman is here to see you."

He paused. "What woman?"

"She said her name is Kim."

Fear gripped him, but he kept his voice neutral. "Did she say anything to you?"

"No, she's really nice."

Kim came up behind Yvette. Years of long-buried memories threatened to crush him. Why hadn't she changed? She was just as beautiful as when his father had married her over ten years ago. She made sixty look like a gift—her silver hair touching her shoulders, her tailored suit complimenting her figure. She forced a smile, he knew she could smile easily but rarely smiled around him anymore. "You look so much better. Have you made your decision?"

"I'm getting married," he said in a flat tone.

The smile disappeared and confusion replaced it. "What? I thought—"

He held up a hand. "You don't need to think. You just need to leave."

"I was wrong. I can't tell you how awful I feel about everything. I know I was selfish because I couldn't handle your illness and a part of me was jealous of how your father worried about you all the time. I almost felt as though there was three of us in the marriage when I wanted him all to myself. I should have been there for you when Tracy left and you couldn't work for a while and all the things you suffered through. I know you may not forgive me now, but I hope you will one day." She took a hesitant step toward him. "I'm glad that you'll have someone by your side."

He gritted his teeth. "That's not why I'm getting married."

Yvette frowned. "By his side for what?"

Kim sent Yvette a nervous glance then stared at Nate astonished. "Doesn't she know?"

"Know what?"

She turned to Yvette. "Nate has cancer."

Chapter 14

Yvette sat quietly in her room. Now it all made sense: the nose bleeds (she hadn't believed he'd cut his finger in Paris), the sleepless nights, the fevers, the dizziness. He was truly sick. The entire time she was playing make-believe he was dying right in front of her. She felt ill.

Nate knocked softly on the door then entered. "Can I talk to you?"

She shrugged, not trusting herself to speak.

"I'm sorry you found out this way."

"I bet you're sorry I found out at all," she said bitterly.

"I didn't want it to be a factor in your decision."

"You were afraid I wouldn't marry you."

"Or that you'd marry me out of pity."

"What's the decision everyone keeps talking about?"

"I need aggressive treatment to fight this particular cancer and they want to know when I'll start. I've decided not to."

She stared at him. "What? Why?"

"I fought twice before. I thought I'd beaten it both times, but I hadn't and I don't want to go through it again. Kim married my father before my diagnosis. They used to call me their matchmaker. I helped her brother out of a situation then introduced her to my father. After I got sick my father's concern for me put a strain on their marriage. He was by my side all the time, always worried about me. And she…" Nate shrugged. "It was hard for her. One doctor said there was nothing he could do for me. When I told my father he refused to believe that." The corner of his mouth quirked in a quick grin. "He made things happen so that I could get the specialist I have now.

"He's been fighting this thing with me for years. She thinks that there's a chance that *this* time I will get better. I don't. I'm not someone special. I've never done anything great with my life, but with you I feel that my life has meaning."

"I don't understand."

"When I die. You'll receive all my money and as my widow no one can dispute that."

"As your widow?" she said, despair making her voice crack. "You're just going to die?"

He smoothed her hair. "Listen, you won't have to take care of me. I have the money for care and—"

Yvette covered her ears. "I don't want to hear this."

He removed her hands. "I need you to," he said, sounding desperate. "I've been trying to beat death for years and I'm not running anymore. I want to live in the moment. In you I see life and I want you to live the life you dream. Just think about it."

"Okay, I've thought about it."

He looked uneasy yet hopeful. "You have?"

"Yes. If you get the treatment, I'll marry you."

The hope in his eyes died. "I'm not having any treatments."

"Then we'll just stay friends."

"No, we won't. I don't want you as a friend."

"Fine," she said in a hollow voice, lowering her gaze.

He lifted her chin and forced a smile. "You're

seeing too much in this. I want you to know that I've been looking at this from all sides and I've made my decision. There's no one I would want to leave all my money to other than you."

"Then you'll have to find someone else."

"Why?"

"Because I love you."

"I love you, too."

"Then have the treatment. Do whatever it takes."

He glanced down.

"Aren't you going to say anything?"

He looked at her with anguish. "I can't say what you want me to."

"You'd rather drop dead and give me all your money than stay alive and live with me?"

"It's not like that. I'm tired. This is my third battle and I'm tired of wondering if I'll make it. You know how freeing it is to stop worrying? To stop striving and trying to achieve? It's a relief. I am not afraid of death."

"You'd rather welcome death than fight for life?"

"Death has been knocking on my door for a long time."

"That doesn't mean you have to open it."

His eyes filled with tears but he dropped his gaze before she could see them. "So you won't marry me?"

Yvette bit her trembling lip. "I can't."

"Even if I told you that the money—"

"I don't care about the money! Why don't you believe me? If you spent every last cent on getting better—"

"But there's no guarantee. What's the point in spending money, time and energy on something you can't control? How do you think it makes me feel to think of leaving you with a memory of me in treatments instead of lazing on a beach?"

"At least I would know that you tried."

"And failed."

"You could succeed."

"The odds are against me."

"But there's still a chance."

"A small one."

"But it's there all the same."

He flashed a weak smile. "You're still so stubborn."

"So are you." Her voice fell. "Please, Nate."

He shook his head, then stood. "I'm sorry," he said and meant it but it didn't help. "At least we had fun."

"Yes, that's something to remember."

He opened his mouth then closed it, knowing there was no more to say. He sighed as though the weight of the world had fallen on his shoulders and left.

Yvette stared at the door for several minutes then began to pack. Moments later she entered the living room with her luggage. Kim sat alone on the couch. "He went for a walk."

"It's okay," Yvette said. "I don't need to see him."

"I didn't mean to ruin things for you."

"You didn't do anything. You can't ruin what isn't real."

Kim jumped to her feet, distressed. "Please don't make that mistake. What you have is real and wonderful. Don't throw it away. Nate can be stubborn, but I know you could bend him a little. Perhaps if you gave it some more time…"

"No," Yvette said, wanting to believe Kim's words, but not allowing herself to. "I was trying to make a wish come true that wasn't meant to be." Yvette placed an envelope on the table then put a leash on James. She took one last look around then walked to the door facing the reality that her dream had come to an end.

"She's gone," Kim told Nate when he returned. "But she left you a note."

Nate raced over to the table and ripped the envelope open. The keys to the apartment and a check fell out. There was no note, no words, just a check made out to him for the remainder of the money she hadn't spent. He fell into a chair as though he'd been punched. She didn't want to be with him and didn't want anything from him not even his money.

"What did she say?" Kim asked.

Nate crumpled the check in his fist. "Goodbye."

The moment Yvette stepped into the foyer of her building, Mrs. Cantrell opened her door. She noticed Yvette's bags and smiled. "You're back from your vacation. My Arthur won't stop talking about how wonderful your date was. Come in. I think…"

"Not today, Mrs. Cantrell," Yvette said, dragging herself to the stairs. "I'm really tired."

"You just need some food."

"I just need some sleep, thank you." She slowly climbed the stairs and walked to her apartment. Elliot peeked his head out.

"So you're finally back."

"Yes." She opened her door.

"I baked—"

"No." Yvette walked inside, dropped her luggage in front of the door then fell face-first on the couch. She couldn't even cry. She felt too hollow inside for tears. She glanced up and saw *On the Town* magazine where she had left it on her coffee table. Suddenly anger gripped her as she thought of how empty and stupid her wishes had been. She leaped up, gathered all her magazines and threw them in the garbage. Then she called Rania.

"It's all a sham, isn't it? You don't make dreams come true. You just turn them into nightmares."

Rania replied to Yvette's anger in a calm voice. "What are you talking about?"

"Nate asked me to marry him."

"That's wonderful."

"And then I find out he's dying of cancer."

Rania paused. "Did he ask for a prenup?"

"What?"

"What will happen to the money after he dies?"

For a moment Yvette was too stunned to speak. "Who cares? He's sick."

"And that bothers you?"

"Of course it does! Why wouldn't it?"

"Because you've never been really interested in men and this sounds like a great solution. You marry him for a few months and then he dies and you inherit his money. I thought you wanted lots of money, but the man didn't matter."

"I was wrong. You tricked me."

"I didn't trick anyone."

"I don't mean you personally, I mean this whole stupid club. It promised things it can't deliver."

"It gave you *exactly* what you wanted. You're the one who changed the rules."

"This is why I prefer animals to people. Animals don't have hidden agendas, animals don't toy with your emotions, animals are genuine and they don't hurt you."

"Funny how you're always talking about how people have hurt you, but have you ever considered that you might be hurting him?"

"What do you mean?"

"The moment he didn't do something you wanted him to, you left him. Does that show true love?"

"But I want him to get well."

"What about what he wants? Doesn't that matter, too? Is it wrong for him to want to spend his life with you on his terms? He made himself vulnerable the moment he asked you to marry him. He doesn't know how long he has to live, but he does know that he wants to spend that time with you. You can't always be the one in charge, Yvette. People aren't like animals that you can force to follow your rules. You have to give something, too. You can love animals unconditionally, but it's time you learn to love people the same way."

The moment Yvette hung up the phone she covered her eyes. Perhaps Rania was right. Maybe if she talked to Nate some more they could compromise. She decided to drive to Diana's apartment. She knocked on the door rehearsing what she would say to Nate when she saw him, but his sister opened the door instead. "Oh, you're back," Yvette said awkwardly.

"Yes."

"Is Nate home?"

Diana shook her head. "No, he just left."

"Do you know when he'll be back?"

"He's not coming back."

Chapter 15

Over next several months Yvette buried herself in work. She kept to herself, leaving Greg to handle clients while she dealt with the dogs. She never came out from behind the curtain until the end of the day. Her routine was made up of work and home. She didn't return phone calls or e-mails. She didn't want to talk to anyone. One evening, while she was teaching James a new trick, someone knocked on the door. She sighed, glancing briefly outside as the late-autumn wind beat at her window, then answered. Bernard stood there with a large canvas.

"What are you doing here?" She gripped the door handle, stunned.

"Sorry it's a little overdue."

"It doesn't matter."

"May I come in?"

Yvette stepped aside and he entered. He glanced around, impressed. "Nice place."

"Thanks."

He rested the canvas against the wall then bent down to pet James.

"What are you doing here?"

"Nate's sister, Diana, gave me your address."

"That's not what I meant."

"I know." He sat then said in French, "I'm not the enemy."

Yvette stood and faced him, unmoved. "There's nothing for us to say."

"At least look at the painting."

"There's no point."

"Please," he said softly.

She reluctantly tore off the paper and stared at the finished portrait. It showed Nate as her valet and she as his mistress. A flood of memories threatened to come forth, but she pushed them back. "It's beautiful, but it represents a time of make-believe and that time is over."

"I met Nate when he was in the hospital. I

worked at the hospital doing art therapy. He was one of my best students. He had the heart of a true artist, intense, passionate with an eye for detail."

"I know how talented he is."

"Through him I was able to meet his family when they came to visit. I got to know his father and his aunt and his cousin."

Yvette made an impatient motion with her hand. "What does what you're telling me have to do with anything?"

"Have you been to the Kerner mansion?"

"Yes."

"Have you seen a large painting of Cathleen with her mother?"

"You painted that?"

"Yes. I got to spend a lot of time with Cathleen when her mother wasn't around, which wasn't often, but it was often enough to allow me to fall in love with her."

"With Cathleen? Why didn't you say anything?"

"I wasn't sure how she felt about me. I was just a poor artist working with patients at a hospital. I didn't feel I had anything to offer her. She was young and pretty and rich. What would she like about me, I thought. So once I finished my contract at the hospital, I left without a word.

Although I thought about her often, I felt certain I had made the right choice. Until I saw you."

"Me? Why?"

"You dared to live life fully and freely. You enjoyed every moment not caring about the next day or the next moment. You lived without fear. I watched you show Nate that same fearlessness. And I knew I wanted to be fearless, too." He pulled out a ring. "She may say 'no' or she may say 'yes' but that doesn't matter to me anymore because at least she'll know that I love her."

"Now may not be the right time," Yvette said, thinking of Lewis.

Bernard shrugged. "*Now* is the only time we have."

Cathleen sat on the edge of the waterfall sculpture, staring blindly at her reflection in the water. The day was unusually warm for autumn, the rays of the sun pounded her back but inside she still felt cold. Lewis's betrayal still stung, but what hurt her more were her last words to Nate and his abrupt departure. She hadn't been able to reach him—no one had, (except his father who wouldn't tell anyone where he was) but when she got the chance she'd make it up to him.

He was her cousin and her friend and she'd been unfair. She'd been flattered by Lewis but she hadn't truly loved him. It had taken her an agonizing month to realize that and face how foolish and blind she'd been.

"You look like a painting."

She turned when she heard the voice then jumped to her feet. "Bernard!" All her sorrow disappeared as she remembered the months she'd spent with him. She'd missed his face and his easy grin, but most of all their walks together down the hospital corridor where she's shared her worries about Nate and her relationship with her mother and he'd listened without judgment. Then one day he'd left without saying goodbye.

"Nate's not here."

"I know. I didn't come to see him. I flew all the way from Paris to ask you a question."

She frowned confused. "What?"

He got down on one knee and held out a black box. "I should have asked you this over a year ago, but I didn't have the courage. I love you, will you marry me?"

"Absolutely not!" Penny said, coming through the patio doors. "I want you to leave."

"He's not going anywhere, Mother, because I will marry him." She turned to Bernard. "But he will have to wait."

Bernard's hands trembled as he placed the ring on her finger. "As long as you want me to."

"My God!" Penny cried. "You have nothing to offer my daughter." She looked at Cathleen. "He's only after your money."

"No, he's not. I've learned the difference between flattery and true love."

"But we don't know anything about him. How old are you?"

They shared a glance then Cathleen replied, "Thirty-five."

She'd made a big mistake. She shouldn't have come to New York and she certainly shouldn't have come here. Yvette sat inside the taxi, tugged on her jean skirt, which covered her last pair of new stockings. She took a deep breath. *She had to do this. She had to see him again.* There were so many things she wanted to tell him and so many things she wanted to know. Kim hadn't been able to tell her anything about where Nate had disappeared to over the last few months, but all she knew was that he'd returned home the past two weeks.

Yvette looked out at the building in front of her. It wasn't an ordinary house but it wasn't a mansion, either. It was too small. It was a lot like Nate—unassuming, but grand; stately yet homey. It rested on acres of land dusted white by a brief winter snow. She glanced down at James, who sat in his carrier. "It's now or never." She opened the door.

The taxi driver unloaded her luggage. Yvette paid and tipped him. She heard the taxi drive away as she made her way up the front steps. She knocked on the door. A man answered but it wasn't Nate. He was a tidy-looking man with a stocky build and dark eyes. He took her bags before she could introduce herself. "Follow me," he said.

"Don't you want to know who I am?"

He motioned to a framed sketch in the hallway. "Is that you?"

Yvette blinked surprised. "Yes."

"That's what I thought." He led her into the living room. "Please, take a seat. You can let James out."

"You know about James, too? Has he told you about me?"

He only smiled. "Please, take a seat. I'll tell him you're here."

Yvette let James out of his carrier, but she didn't sit down. She couldn't. She was too excited to see him. Had he been eating well, sleeping well? The moment he came into the room she knew the answer. He hadn't.

He looked terrible. His eyes were red and his face unshaven. He looked tired, but managed a sly grin. "Hello."

She ran up to him. "I don't care how much

time you have. I want to be with you. I understand if—"

"Yvette."

"I have to be by your side. I won't leave you alone."

"Yvette."

"And I want you to know that—"

He grabbed her shoulders. "Yvette. Listen."

"Yes?"

"Don't worry. I just didn't sleep last night. I got a call from my doctor."

Her heart stopped. "And?"

He began to smile.

She stared at him in numb astonishment. "You're cancer-free?"

He smiled and nodded. "Yes, I'm in remission."

She threw her arms around him, nearly knocking him over. "I missed you."

He hugged her back so tightly she thought her ribs would break, but she didn't care. She pressed her head against his chest and listened to his heart beat, its strong rhythmic motion making her want to weep with gratitude.

"Come. Let's sit down." He led her to the couch, but not before scooping James up and patting him on the head. In the excitement of seeing Nate, he'd had a little accident but only the valet noticed and discreetly cleaned it up. James licked Nate's face.

Yvette snuggled close, not wanting any distance between them. "What made you change your mind?"

He sighed with remembered pain and put James down. "The check. When I opened that envelope and saw it, I knew you didn't want or need my money. At first I was angry. That's why I left. Then I realized that I had relied on it a bit too much. I always used it to get what I wanted. I thought it was my money that got you and thought I would use it to keep you, but you made me see that I was wrong."

"I was wrong, too. I may not always agree with you, but I'll always stand by you."

He gathered her close. "You don't have a choice because I don't plan on letting you go. You made me want to live again."

She rested her head on his shoulder then saw a familiar face in a photo. She sat up and reached for the picture.

Nate looked over at her. "That's my dad with his two sisters when they were young." He pointed. "Aunt Penny hasn't changed much and that's Aunt Maggie. She's sort of the black sheep of the family. Every few months she likes to dress up like a bag lady and pay homeless people for their pets, especially dogs. She'll then have the pets cleaned and groomed and either keep them or put them up for adoption. She's rescued lots of dogs this way. You two have a lot in common."

Yvette gripped the side of the frame. "I already met her."

Nate raised his eyebrows. "You did?"

"She was the lady I told you about. The one who abandoned James." She shook her head in wonder. "It's almost as if everything in my life changed the moment I met her. It's almost as if—"

"As if what?"

It was all magic. But Yvette was too practical to believe in magic. "It was meant to be."

Nate drew her close. "I know it was. I hope you'll meet her again one day. You have the same sense of style. I mean, look at what she's wearing."

He didn't need to point it out. Yvette already saw it. Maggie wore a straw hat, purple dress and familiar lace stockings…

Tyson Braddock was not a man to be denied....

Second Chance, Baby

Book #3 in The Braddocks: Secret Son

A.C. ARTHUR

Except for one passion-filled night, Ty and Felicia Braddock's
marriage has been cold for years. Now Felicia is pregnant.
Unwilling to raise her baby with an absentee workaholic
father, Felicia wants a divorce. Ty convinces her to give him
another chance. But as they rediscover the passion they'd lost,
will it be enough to make them a family?

THE BRADDOCKS

SECRET SON

power, passion and politics are all in the family

Available the first week of October wherever books are sold.

KIMANI
ROMANCE™

www.kimanipress.com

KPACA0841008

Was her luck running out?

GAMBLE ON
Love

The second title in The Ladies of Distinction…

MICHELLE MONKOU

"Black American Princess" Denise Dixon has met
her match in sexy, cynical Jaden Bond. But as their
relationship heats up, she knows their days are numbered
before her shameful family secrets are revealed.

THE LADIES *of* DISTINCTION:

They've shared secrets, dreams and heartaches.
And when it comes to finding love, these sisters
always have each other's backs.

Available the first week of October wherever books are sold.

KIMANI™
ROMANCE

www.kimanipress.com   KPMM0861008

She was beautiful, bitter and bent on revenge!

Tender SECRETS

ANN CHRISTOPHER

Vivica Jackson has vowed vengeance on the wealthy
Warners for causing her family's ruin—but that's before
she experiences Andrew Warner's devastating charm.
After the would-be enemies share a night of fiery passion,
each is left wanting more. But will her undercover
deception and his dark family secret lead to a not-so-
happy ending to their love story?

Available the first week of October wherever books are sold.

KIMANI™
ROMANCE

www.kimanipress.com   KPAC0871008

What Matters Most

ARABESQUE®

ESSENCE **BESTSELLING AUTHOR**

DONNA HILL

Temptation

Liaisons, Noelle Maxwell's chic romantic retreat,
is the ultimate fantasy. But there is no idyllic
escape from her past, and Noelle has vowed to
uncover the truth behind the mysterious death of
her husband. Yet the only man she can trust is
a stranger whose explosive sexuality awakens
desire—and fear. Because Cole Richards has a
secret, too....

**"Riveting and poignant, this novel will
transport readers to new heights
of literary excellence."**
**—*Romantic Times BOOKreviews*
on *Temptation***

Coming the first week of October wherever books are sold.

ARABESQUE®

www.kimanipress.com

KPDH1081008